A PARTY OF CERTAINTIES

ON BEHALF OF DEATH, BOOK 3

E.G. STONE

TARNEY BRAE CREATIVE ENDEAVOURS

For my Grandad, from whom much inspiration for this book came.

TAX FREE

Have you ever felt nothing? And I don't mean depression. I don't mean those days where it's hard to get out of bed because the world is weighing on your shoulders, although to be fair, working for Death means that I felt that on occasion. I don't mean boredom or apathy, preventing you from getting up to choose the next movie. Or even just tiredness that makes thinking really difficult.

No, I mean nothing.

No pain.

No joy.

No interest.

No boredom.

Hunger and thirst? Nada.

Considering the fact that I was sitting around a poker table with a bunch of slightly corporeal souls, I should have perhaps been feeling something. Their time in, well, purgatory? The waiting room? Some sort of in between place between the here and now in the afterwards, gave them a whole lot of time for playing cards, dealing in favours. Which made them very good at poker. I should have been quaking in my shoes, afraid to lose. Especially considering that to my right sat Al Capone and to my left sat Genghis Khan. Across from me sat a woman whose eyes watched me like some sort of cat after prey. She told me her name, but I didn't remember it. The other two called her Mata Hari.

I wasn't nervous. Or afraid. Or anything, really.

See, all these people were dead. Long dead. I was playing with their ghosts, I suppose. I was not dead. Far from it, actually. In fact, given my current situation, I couldn't actually die at all. This was due to a rather complicated set of circumstances in which I had found myself after being shot in a park. See, I had been shot—whether I had been shot fatally is an entirely different question—and met Death. He offered me a job as his marketing agent and public relations manager. Considering who he was, I saw the need. So I accepted. This got me into a whole bunch of situations with my rock troll assistant Yolanda, my air elemental marketing trainee Agravane, some very angry supernatural beings, almost a week with Machiavelli and a half-giantess and the time travelling journalist, and here I was.

Soulless.

Feeling nothing. Nothing at all.

Death had lost my soul. It was a whole problematic accident that had to do with time travel and inevitability and other theories that I don't understand.

The point was that Death, after making me immortal in the present had lost my soul in the past, meaning that I couldn't die even if I were killed. Being soulless also meant that I couldn't feel anything. According to Yolanda, I was becoming rather more like a psychopathic killer than the slightly grumpy boss she had come to appreciate so much.

I suppose I should have been bothered by that statement. I wasn't.

Of course, if I wanted to stop being an emotionless, potentially dangerous person who would turn into a zombie that required orders to do anything, including sleep and eat, then I needed a soul. Considering that mine was lost, and even Death didn't know where to find it, I needed a temporary solution.

Hence, poker.

"Raise you a favour." Mata Hari threw some chips into the centre. She blinked languidly at me, possibly seeing if I was going to blush. I just considered my cards.

We were playing for different stakes than standard poker. The three opponents of mine were dead. They had no need for such things as money. But they did trade in favours. If I won, then I would get temporary usage of their soul. Now, I knew how to play poker in the theory. I had seen enough James Bond movies to understand the concept. I even had a fairly stunning poker face, considering that I felt nothing and showed no emotion ever. The only problem was, I had never actually played poker. So I was doing poorly.

"Too rich for my blood," Genghis Khan said. I

wondered if he were actually speaking English, or if it was just the fact that all the dead were universally understood, because I was fairly certain that that sort of slang hadn't been around during the Mongol Empire. He folded his cards, sitting back in his chair with a displeased expression. He had lost spectacularly already, being down to his last favour. Mata Hari was doing slightly worse than I was, having played aggressively the whole game with little regard to actually winning. This might have surprised me if I had known more about her history apart from her being a universally acknowledged spy. I just assumed that she wasn't a very good player.

Al Capone called on Mata Hari. He gave me a sideways glance and smirked. "For a living guy, you're kinda boring. You got nothing to say? No stories? Come on, Cal Thorpe, give us some entertainment."

"Raise," I said, throwing my chips into the centre. "I am unsure as to what you would find entertaining."

Mata Hari folded her hand, narrowing her eyes at me. She flicked her brown hair over her shoulder and crossed her legs under the table, shifting her posture ever so slightly. Capone straightened in his chair, considering. The other two were out. By my understanding of the game and what favours each player had left, this was an indication that it was down to Capone and I. If I won, I got use of his soul. If I lost, I would owe him enough favours to keep me employed by the former gangster for nearly a year. Neither option bothered me, nor interested me.

"Call." Capone narrowed his eyes at me and ran his

hands over each other, fiddling with the cufflinks at his wrist. "You work for Death. That's the only reason you're in this game. Anyone who works for Death has to have some interesting stories. At least tell us you've met his wife? You know, Life?"

"I have met Life." I threw my cards over, showing them to the table. Capone whistled and deposited his on the table also, leaning back and snarling at me.

"You've been playing mediocre all night long. It comes down to the final hand and what do you got? A royal straight flush. You are either superbly lucky, or you've got some tricks up your sleeve." Al Capone shook his head, then stood and held out his hand. "Congratulations, Cal Thorpe. You have won the use of my soul for precisely a month."

"Thank you," I said, also standing. Capone looked at me and held out his hand a little farther, shaking it and raising his eyebrows expectantly. "Oh, you mean for me to take possession now. Forgive me, I did not understand the implication."

I took Capone's hand, and some sort of something happened. One moment, I was feeling nothing, and the next moment, I was feeling everything. I was elated at having won at poker, a little terrified of Genghis Khan and even more terrified—and also slightly attracted—at the site of Mata Hari's glaring eyes. I felt hunger from the fact that I hadn't eaten for two days, a little tired from having been up for a while playing the card game. I still couldn't feel as fully as I had done before losing my soul, but I felt a little more human.

I also felt Al Capone residing inside my head, his

thoughts and emotions stronger than mine. I couldn't quite put my finger on the emotion that he was feeling at the moment, but it was beyond interest, into the territory of self-satisfaction. It was as if he was feeling…

"Smug?" I asked out loud, pushing my glasses up the bridge of my nose. "Why in the world would you be feeling smug?"

Somehow both inside my mind and without, an image of Capone appearing in my vision as clearly as if he were once again a ghost beside me. He looked the same as ever: average height, a little heavy, brown hair, scar on his face. Except he was wearing a grin that could have terrified some of the monsters I'd met. He spoke. "Are you kidding me? I haven't looked this good in ages. You're a little skinny, but you've got actual hands and flesh. You can go places. Do things. You know how long I have been at that table, trading favours in the hope that something more interesting will happen? And then Death comes around and asks if will let one of his people join. And now, I get to go back into the *real world*. Temporarily, of course, and not under my own control, but I want a drink like you wouldn't believe."

"Food, I can understand. I am hungry. Oddly. But, visiting the mortal realms and doing things like going out for a drink, that will have to wait. I have a bunch of new clients to deal with, not to mention Life and Death foisted their family reunion party planning on to me. It's in a week." With that, I waved goodbye to a confused looking Genghis Khan and an angry Mata

Hari, turned around and strode out of the doorway that was my entrance to the ether.

Death had opened this doorway in the heart of my office, saying it would be open long enough for me to go and return. When I had left, my office was as neat and tidy as ever, the desk of my assistant being only slightly less neat than my own, considering that it was covered with tiny geode's and a bag of popcorn. My own desk was terrifyingly clean, any papers organised within an inch of their life, my computer up to date and all of my tasks done. Across the office was the slightly beat up desk of Agravane, the air elemental or aurai I had rescued a while back. He had become some sort of trainee marketing agent and errand boy for the office. I was a little shocked at the neatness of my desk, considering that I was, generally speaking, a messy person, but I was more shocked by the banner that hung across the office, the words *Hooray for Cal's Soul* written in sloppy letters across it. Beneath the banner, Yolanda stood with a ridiculous party had on her bald head.

Yolanda was a rock troll, exiled from her people long before I had met her. She was possessed of greyish green skin, wide yellow eyes, strangely white teeth, and was built along the lines of a rugby player. So seeing her in a party hat was a little shocking. What was more shocking was that Agravane was also wearing a party hat, though his looked as though it had been forced upon him.

I frowned. Shoved my hands in my pockets. "What is all this?"

Yolanda almost squealed and clapped her hands excitedly. "You are back! I mean, back in the office, too, but with a soul! Now you can get back to being our grumpy boss."

"I think what she means is that we were both tired of the emotionless stare we kept getting from you these last few days, which is why your desk looks like it's been attacked by brownies determined on cleaning it within an inch of its life. Comparatively, having you back and grumbling at us is a far more agreeable option." Agravane narrowed his eyes and slouched even more, his annoyingly good looks suiting the expression perfectly. "You did win the use of the soul, did you not?"

"Yes, I did," I said with a sniff. In my vision, though apparently invisible to everyone else, Al Capone snickered. He tugged at the sleeves of his suit, walking around my office as though it were his. I felt his arrogance and that same annoying smugness rising.

"Should we ask whose soul you're using?" Yolanda ventured tentatively, scuffing her shoe on the floor. "I mean, just in case it might affect…you."

"Go on, Cal," Al Capone said, stepping over to the window and looking out onto the grounds of death's estate in elsewhere. He turned around and faced the room, appraising it. "Put them out of their misery. Just tell them."

I pinched the bridge of my nose beneath my glasses. "Al Capone," I said to Yolanda and Agravane, deciding that it was perhaps not the best moment to begin talking to myself—even if there was actually an entity inside my head. "I am playing host to the most notorious gangster in American history. There, are you happy?"

Agravane snickered. He went over to his desk and sat, propping his heels on the edge and brushing lint off his trousers. "Seems a perfect match to me. After all, we have a family reunion to plan, and Al Capone sure could throw a great party."

I sat down at my desk and pulled out the guest list, already feeling a bit of dread. Muted dread, given that my soul was who knows where and the one I was using was just temporary, but dread none the same. After all, I was just a marketing agent, and I was walking around with a notorious gangster in my head. What could possibly go wrong? Well, let me rephrase. What could possibly go wrong this time?

DEATH AND TAXES

orking for Death means that I tend to come into contact with fairly terrifying beings at regular intervals. Planning a party for Death's family—some of whom I had met and was suitably terrified of, and others whom I hadn't met and was still terrified of—hadn't struck me as something to be avoided when Death first gave me the assignment. However, I now had access to a soul. Granted, it was Al Capone and therefore my fear response seemed to be unusually low, but at the thought of having Death's family—some of the most powerful supernatural entities in the universe—in one place—I will admit to panic.

The days of planning the party involved a lot of me muttering to myself and trying to figure out ways in which to prevent things from going wrong. I'd been given a list of very short notations on each family member from Death, stating whether or not someone had a food allergy or whether two aunts or uncles could be seated together. I had been told to hire a photographer and just the thought of that had me scowling for about an hour, according to Yolanda.

I had informed her that the scowl was because the family portraits were sure to do really terribly on all of the social media platforms. People were already afraid enough of Death, but a full portrait of him and his family was enough to send even the strongest and sanest running for the hills. Not that my marketing strategy for Death was to paint him as a being of sunshine and smiles.

Still, I did manage to do all of the necessary party things, and on the day of the event itself, Death's estate was opened up to caterers and people who were setting up the tent and tables, two photographers—oddly enough, these were creatures of the same lineage as Doc Graveltoes, a strange gremlin goblin thing that fancied itself a healer—and many more. I oversaw the movements of Death's heirloom silver to the tables from his grand palatial mansion, a building that seemed to be a cross between Victorian and Tudor style, with ivy of a muted silver climbing the walls, power and beauty in the very stones. I didn't think to ask who Death had inherited his silvers from. I didn't want to know. I had the caterers setting up off to one side, the brownies that were doing the cooking happy to stay out of the way.

By the time 4 o'clock came around, I had imbibed 3 cups of coffee, no food, and was thoroughly tired of listening to Al Capone rant in my head about the unsuitability of having various alcohols placed next to one another at the bar. I sank into one of the chairs at a table of solid cherry, feeling weariness for the first time in several days. Then it occurred to me that I hadn't slept in rather while.

But you know what? I had put together one really, really good party.

And I was pleased with the efforts.

"You have done well," Death said, peering behind me like some sort of ghost. Had I been more connected to the current soul inhabiting my body, or possessed of a soul more in tune with the ability to feel an appropriate sense of fear, then Death would have scared the living daylights out of me. As it was, I propped my head in my hand, pushed my glasses up my nose and appraised my boss.

Death, as usual, was wearing clothes that put most people to shame. He was a bit of a dandy. Today, he was wearing a pinstripe three-piece suit in black and grey, a red silk cravat hid his neck, a matching pocket square in his left breast pocket, patent leather shoes, and a cane of ebony with a silver skull at its head. A bit over-dramatic, but given the guest list, it seemed to work.

"Am I going to be expecting any destruction today? Is your estate going to fall to pieces? Will I be blamed for any of it?" They were not the questions that I had intended on asking, but they were the ones that came out. I scowled deeper.

Death chuckled and took the chair beside me, tapping his cane on the grass. "Still having difficulties getting Mr. Capone's soul under control?"

"He had me interrogating the whiskey vendor for

twenty minutes," I said. I coughed nervously and looked at Death, knowing the answer to my question before I even asked it. "Has there been any news of... my own soul?"

"No." Death looked around and appraised the scene. His estate in the Lands of Silence, his realm in Elsewhere, was made up of the flora that thrived in the whole realm. The silver grey colour of the ivy was the most common, with grass of a lighter mist shade, the trees sporting leaves that were almost blue in their grey, darker threads spreading through the trunks of the trees and into some of the flowers. It was a land that the average onlooker would call monochrome, but I had come to appreciate that there were distinct and fascinating variations in the place. It was not well inhabited by animals, at least not those you would see in any realms of the living, and I had only encountered a couple of them, but there was life there. It was beautiful in its own way. And if I did say so myself, the wooden tables and artful lawn decorations, the shine of the silver and the gleaming white of the tablecloths all contrasted nicely to create a simply stunning party.

I was really good at my job.

"Okay," I said, trying to hide my disappointment at the lack of news. I wasn't surprised. The whole reason I was borrowing Al Capone's soul for a while was to do with the fact that mine was really nowhere to be found. Not even Death seemed to be able to locate it. "You will let me know if you find something, won't you?"

"You have my word," Death said, inclining his head. He blinked slowly, which was a little disturbing given that his eyes were simply empty pits, and staring into them was like looking into the abyss. Death's skin was wreathed in black, so dark that it seemed to produce its own shadows, a trail of his power surrounding him. He gave me one last look, then flicked his gaze to where Al Capone was floating incorporeal he beside me, his own shoes barely touching the tops of the grass. "Do be careful with this one, Cal. He is more dangerous than you expect."

"Well, my other options were Genghis Khan or Mata Hari. You set up the game, this is the result." There was that flatness in my tone again, a tinge of emotionlessness as Al Capone and diverted his attention from me to somewhere else. I coughed pointedly and felt the connection again, his soul bound to me. I should probably try harder to contain him, to control him, but I had been planning a party and I hadn't slept for four days. None of which would kill me, considering I couldn't be killed, but eventually I could be worn down.

"Interesting." Death did not elaborate on that comment, which didn't really surprise me. My boss was nothing if not reticent. He rose from the chair and without a backwards glance, walked away to where people were starting to arrive, magnificent vehicles pulling up to the drive. There was a Lamborghini that disgorged Death's wife, Life, a being so beautiful that it was hard to look at her, so terrifying that touching her could reduce a person to cinders, so enthralling that you wanted to try it anyways. Life and I didn't particularly get along.

Behind the Lamborghini was a horse-drawn carriage, led by four horses in colours that did not occur in the natural world. It stopped and the door opened, revealing a being that was petite, so diminutive I might've called her a fairy, if her presence did not seem to take up every ounce of space that was available. A moment later, a car appeared out of nowhere, instantly recognisable and utterly ridiculous. I recognised the owner of this vehicle and decided that I might as well go mingle, since I didn't really want to stick around and wait for Life to approach me, or for Yolanda to come and hide behind me, her natural terror of the powerful beings here leading her to a quiet and trembling afternoon.

"Ah, Cal! I see you still haven't found your soul," Time said, walking towards me. Time wore a pair of slacks and a white shirt, smirking. I wasn't sure if I liked Time any more than I was fond of Life, but at least had a feeling he wouldn't try to send me back to fourteen ninety-four again. "Oh, Al Capone, a good choice. The 1930s were fascinating. So much going on."

"I like this guy," Al Capone said. "He seems to know what's what."

"This whole thing is your fault. But, it doesn't matter. What matters is...did you really arrive at a DeLorean?" I pointed at the car, which was disgorging strange amounts of fog, as if Time had just driven off the movie set. Time chuckled.

"One must appreciate a certain sense of humour. And I've been told that mine requires improving. So here I am." Time spread his arms and grinned widely. I exchanged a glance with Al, who shrugged.

"Oh yes, because that's just what we need. Time with a sense of humour." As one, all three of us turned to face the newcomer. Agravane was walking towards us, carrying a glass of some sort of wine, raising his eyebrows skeptically at Time. My employee stopped at my shoulder, taking up a sort of protective stance as we faced a down and being that could tear me into itty-bitty pieces without blinking.

"I thought I gave you and Yolanda the afternoon off. Yolanda said she would be coming to the party later, but I thought you had…other plans?" It wasn't that I didn't want Agravane there. I actually found the aurai to be quite interesting to talk with. He had some intriguing views and experiences about the balance between Life and Death, mostly built from his time with the Order of Silence, a zealotous cult dedicated to the balance of the universe. However, Agravane was also, well, aggravating. He had a dark sense of humour. and very little filter since I had rescued him from a place where he had no choice but to filter everything he said. I kept waiting for the pendulum to swing back, but it looked like the bluntness was here to stay. Which was not terribly useful at a party.

"I thought I might attend. Maybe get some interesting pictures for the social media accounts." Agravane held up his phone and waggled it, taking a sip of the wine with his other hand. Well, considering that I was training him to be a full marketing agent, I couldn't really complain with that argument. Besides, Agravane was strangely, stupidly protective of me, and it would be nice not to feel super threatened by everything that I was going to be having a conversation with. It was better than having Yolanda cower behind me, a strange experience from a creature who is almost three feet taller than me.

"Oh do take my picture," Time said, posing with the DeLorean. Agravane raised his brows at me and I shrugged. But he dutifully snapped a few pictures, showing them to Time for his approval. Time nodded, smiled, and spun on his heel, disappearing in a blink.

"I think he might scare me more than Death," Agravane said. He stared at the spot where Time had been. "I mean, I know that Death can end me with a single thought, but Time...Time can shape the very movement of the universe. And he knows things that happened before they do, and somehow makes them our choice. I mean, I think he just likes to cause trouble."

"Time seems to run on his own rules. He seems to believe strongly in the choices of people making up the future, and yet everything is also inevitable. Trying to get into an argument with him about philosophy or the future or anything is like herding cats. Cats with chain saws."

I should know, I'd had more than one argument with him.

Agravane nodded at that and took another long sip of his wine.

"Still, it seems like a decent party. I'm not sure why Death wants a family reunion, considering that he can see his family anytime and anywhere he wants. Did you meet his kids yet?" Agravane nodded his head to where Life and Death were standing, talking to the two younger, obviously immortal beings. I spluttered, and Al Capone patted me on the back, his touch barely substantial, but enough to shake me out of the shock of realising that Death and Life had procreated.

"You know what, I'm hungry. I'm gonna go get some food. And stay very far away from pretty much all of these people." At that, I turned and started walking to where the caterers had set up a buffet. Agravane saluted me as I went.

Brownies may not like to be thanked, or really even acknowledged, but they do a spectacular job in cooking. I knew many five-star restaurants back in the mortal realms that could have thoroughly improved their menu with a single brownie at their disposal. As it was, I was happy to avail myself of their cooking while Death mingled with his guests. I filled my plate with a stuffed shell pasta with butternut squash and saffron, a smoked salmon brioche, some sort of tiny truffle thing, and some falafel. I stuffed my mouth full as a walked along the table, looking to see what other options were provided. Even without a soul, which made it difficult to taste things properly and to experience the full joy of good food, I was thoroughly happy at the buffet. Al's mouth was watering too, and he seemed to be thrilled with the choice and food I was making. I gathered that souls didn't actually need to eat, but sharing the experience of eating food was something you didn't forget just because you didn't have a corporeal body connecting you to the world.

"Grab one of those crème brûlée's," Al said, pointing where a collection of ramekins sat. I nodded, my mouth full of the pasta and reached for the dessert. My hand nearly collided with someone else's and I pulled back, mumbling an apology around my food.

The person I encountered looked nothing like one of Death's guests. He didn't have that overwhelming sense of power, or that enthralling presence that many others seemed to have. He was, in a word, completely average. Average height, average looks, average clothes. Frankly, given the fact that I always considered myself completely average too, I was a little relieved. Partly because I thought that I was perhaps slightly more interesting than this person. But also because I wasn't the only one here who was not on par with the immortal beasties that roamed the party.

"You are welcome to have one," the man said, his voice a little nasally, a little drawling, and completely forgettable. "There seems to be plenty."

"Thank you," I said and grabbed crème brûlée. Al drew closer to my shoulder, his muscles seeming to be tense, his jaw grinding together.

"Cal…be careful," Al warned. I waved the guy off; this person before me was someone with whom I could probably get along quite well. He didn't look like he wanted to devour me or kill me or cause me serious harm by sending me back several hundred years in the history. Al rumbled another warning in my ear, this one incoherent and angry.

"I'm Cal Thorpe," I said, holding out my hand and balancing my plate of food with the other. The man showed his own very full plate of food and shrugged an excuse. I lowered my hand. "I am Death's marketing agent, and apparently also his party organiser."

"Ah, so I have you to thank for the food. The last family reunion we had was done in this cavern somewhere in the middle of Elsewhere, the food was absolutely atrocious." Okay, so this guy was a guest. I mean, I had figured as much, but he didn't look like a member of Death's family. He must have seen the question on my face, because he smiled an apology. My hand reached for a stuffed pepper, almost of its own volition.

"Of course, you wouldn't recognise me by face. I am Death's cousin. I'm the Taxman," he said with a smile. I took in his average clothes again, his average looks, his average height, his average expression, and felt the beginnings of fear in the back of my mind. I couldn't tell if this came from me or from Al Capone. I could tell, however, that the stuffed pepper that my right hand was currently lobbing at the tax man was definitely not done by my will.

The pepper hit the taxman square in the chest, ruining his pressed white shirt. Al Capone snarled a victory beside me. "Take that Taxman! You're not gonna get me again."

I took in a breath, forcing my will on Al Capone, pushing him aside and regaining control of my body. "Ah. Well."

"This was my favourite shirt," the Taxman said. He looked at the remains of the stuffed pepper on the ground at his feet, then back up at me. "Someone's going to have to pay for it."

Well, great. My first public outing with Al Capone as my ride along, and things were already going pretty much as expected. Which was to say, not well at all.

TAX DAY

If I had been feeling it all normally, being called to Death's study would have been something like being called to the principal's office. Of course, no principal's office that I knew of was panelled in rosewood, with bookshelves stretching from floor to ceiling, club chairs of worn, warm leather flanking an ever burning fireplace. Frankly, it felt more like a proper English club, a place of refuge and peace, than any study. Then again, I had never actually seen Death do work, so I wasn't entirely sure what his study would require.

As it was on that day, Death stood beside the fireplace, with the Taxman sitting in one of the club chairs, glaring angrily at me. I was still full of the defiant self-righteousness that Al Capone was radiating, standing there with my hands casually in my pockets, my shoulders straight but somehow slouched. It was a stature of unspoken power, the knowledge that I was one of the more powerful beings in the room. I wasn't. I knew this. But for some reason, I could not get rid of that slouch, the one that mirrored Capone, as he stood there beside me.

"Would you care to explain why it is that you threw food at my cousin?" Death asked, brushing some imagined dirt off his lapel. He glanced at me with raised eyebrows, which was a little disturbing given his lack of eyes and eyebrows. Death was, after all, basically shadow covering skull. "This is a grave offence, Cal. You have broken guest protocol."

I swallowed, the first act that felt fully mind since Capone had thrown the stuffed pepper at the taxman. Guest protocol in many places in the moral realms no longer meant anything. Depending on the culture, people did as they pleased. But in Elsewhere, it still held huge amounts of power, sometimes even more than any law. It was almost as unassailable as the reality of Life and Death themselves.

Unfortunately for me, swallowing was about the only acts that I could manage without Al taking control. He spoke for me. "It's on account of him that I went to prison in the first place. It's on account of him that I lost my empire, that I died forgotten."

I closed my eyes and squeeze them shut. I had been killed countless times, had solved a murder on behalf of Death, had travelled through time, and I was not about to let one dead American gangster control my body. I imagined myself reaching out and grabbing hold of the back of Al's neck, squeezing it and forcing him out of control of my body. The apparition beside me hissed and reached back as if to swat away my hand. It wasn't actually there, and any pressure that he exerted on me to remain in charge failed. I was Cal Thorpe, and while I may have been having a really bad day, it was my body. It wasn't just going to let some minor possession make things worse. Once I was fairly certain that Al was contained within a mental cage, I opened my eyes and looked up.

Death was still watching me with brows raised, but the Taxman was looking at me with an open sneer of disdain. "Everyone must pay their taxes, Mr. Capone. It is not my fault that you chose to disregard that."

Al snarled from within the cage, the apparition beside me doing his best to advance on the Taxman. I kept him still. "You have my sincerest apologies," I said, not even a hint of a waver in my voice. Perhaps that was because I had somehow weakened the bond between Al and myself in maintaining control, or perhaps it was because my possession of his soul was only a temporary solution, one meant to keep me from becoming nothing, not one meant to keep me human. "I have only recently acquired the use of Mr. Capone's soul and I am incredibly sorry for losing control long enough for him to…break guest protocol."

"Cal, if it were under any other circumstances, I would be inclined to do absolutely nothing in reprimand. You losing your soul was indeed my fault, and therefore some of the consequences must be mine. However, you have broken guest protocol. You have allowed Mr. Capone to use your body and throw…a stuffed pepper at my cousin. Given the unusual circumstances surrounding the situation, I cannot agree to full reparations. However, I can force you to repay a favour. Death's voice was sombre, more serious than I had heard him in quite some time. For all that he was, well, Death, my boss was usually in generally good cheer. Oh, you would only very rarely hear him laugh, and I myself had only heard him give a dark chuckle every now and again, but he usually bore some sort of half smile and a general disinclination towards maiming and utter chaos. That was more the providence of his wife, who was really and truly terrifying.

To have him turn this solemn tone on to me, to have him declare that I would be repaying one of *his* favours—one of the primary means of currency in Elsewhere—made me more than a little uncomfortable. But, he was right. It was my fault that I hadn't controlled Capone. I hadn't thought it necessary to put such checks into place because we were going to be at a party, and any of the guests could probably squish me with their little fingers. That was why my assistant Yolanda, a rock troll and theoretically quite powerful, was hiding away in our offices instead of at the party as promised, probably watching a movie and eating salted popcorn. That was why Agravane had stood so close, his bizarre protective instinct toward me getting in the way of a healthy dose of respect and fear. It had been mildly relieving to have the mind of, admittedly, a dangerous killer at my disposal. That was obviously a mistake.

"Absolutely," I said, finally managing to pull my hands from my pockets. "I can absolutely fulfil a favour. I mean, I probably wouldn't be able to do the things that Death can do, but I can provide you with all of the skills at my disposal." Granted, that statement was probably not my wisest one, given the circumstances that working for Death usually got me into, but the accusation and the crime were quite serious. Truthfully, Death could easily strip me of Al's soul and leave me in emotionless, mindless creature for eternity and be perfectly justified in his punishment. I'd heard stories of killing people who broke guest protocol. It was a serious breach of honour and order and when you had beings who could level whole cities together, those things were more important than coffee. The favour was potentially dangerous, but in the long run, a far better option. I just hoped it wouldn't involve wrestling dragons or something. I might not of been able to be killed, but I could feel pain.

"Very well," the Taxman said with the air of someone having just dotted the last 'i' and crossed the last 't' on a legal contract. "I accept this exchange as reparation for breaking guest protocol. As it turns out, I have need of someone who has connections to both the mortal realm and the magical nature of Elsewhere. There is someone in Chicago who has been dodging my messages."

Oh, thank goodness, I wasn't going to be wrestling dragons.

"Um…and by dodging messages you mean…?"

The Taxman sniffed, almost disdainfully. "It is a

circumstance of someone not bothering to pay their back taxes. The mortal authorities within the American Internal Revenue Service are unequipped to deal with the situation, given the magical nature of this particular individual. However, I cannot have the authorities of Elsewhere intercede because he resides solely in the mortal realms. Therefore, I require you to go to Chicago and to collect the back taxes that this individual owes."

At the word Chicago, I felt a surge of excitement from Al in the back of my mind, one strong enough to almost break the mental cage that I was keeping him in. I gritted my teeth, shoved my glasses up my nose, and nodded.

"And, if it's not too much trouble to ask, what is the nature of this individual?" It wouldn't do very well to get myself into trouble with some supernatural heavyweight, expecting nothing more than an angry sprite. I had walked into a few too many situations without enough information and I was going to get as much as possible beforehand. Maybe that would make this thing easier. Somehow, I doubted it.

The Taxman shifted in his chair, folding his hands primly. He shifted his eyes to Death. "This is why I had hoped to acquire your services in the matter, Death. The man in question is a fetch."

Now, I had gotten rather more familiar with the creatures of Elsewhere and the magical world during my time there. I had angered vampires on several occasions, had dealt with gremlins and goblins, ghouls, giant hisses, even a Tatzelwurm. But I had absolutely no idea what a fetch was. "Sorry?" I asked. "What is a fetch and when the world does that have to do with Death?"

Death rubbed at the silk necktie around his throat, making a curious humming sound as he considered. "It is been some time since I have had dealings with fetch. Once, Cal, they were my harbingers. My heralds. A fetch is a being that, in common Irish mythologies and practices, is meant to foretell someone's Death, if met under certain circumstances."

I nodded. Irish. That meant Faeries. I think. "So, they're sort of like every scary faerie creature out there?"

Death rubbed his brow and winced at my statement. The Taxman heaved a very loud sigh. "One of these days, Cal, I am going to have to send you to the Faerie courts so that you can learn things properly. A fetch is an unseelie, and…you know, I think that there are perhaps better, more hands-on ways that you can figure this out. When you meet up with this fellow—"

"Dermot. Dermot Green." The Taxman recited the name as if it were on a form in his mind, which, given his nature, it probably was. I wondered if my form was there, and if it said anything about my taxes. I hadn't paid any taxes, but then, I wasn't sure if people working for Death did. Something I would have to ask Yolanda about.

"Yes. When you meet up with Mr. Green, then you can ask him all the pertinent questions you like. It will be useful training for you." Death gave me one of those peculiar smiles, the one that said things were about to get interesting and I probably wasn't going to like it. I didn't like it when he gave me those smiles. They never ended well for me. "As it is, I have other guests to attend to. I suggest that you remain in your office and see what you can do about containing Mr. Capone properly. It wouldn't do to have any more incidents while you are on assignment."

With that ominous statement, Death rose and strode out of the room as though he hadn't just pronounced my doom with the Taxman.

There's a particular type of silence that falls when you are in the vicinity of any sort of bureaucrat. It's more tense than your average post-argument silence, more drawn out than any awkward conversational pause, and highly terrifying. Something to do with things being done in triplicate, I think. Eventually, after apparently appraising me and the mental cage that I kept Mr. Capone in, the Taxman nodded.

"I, too, am going back to the party. I shall meet you at the entrance to Death's lands first thing tomorrow morning. I suggest you be there." And with that even more terrifying pronouncement of doom, the Taxman rose and left, leaving me alone in a very expensive room that Death favoured. It took me about thirty seconds to come to grips with my new reality and get out of there as quickly as possible. As suggested, I headed directly back to the office, weaving through various guests and tables with discarded drinks and food, doing my best to keep my head down. I made it all the way back to the offices before anyone bothered to ask many questions. The pressure inside my head—

the result of—Al doing his best to escape from the mental cage, was enough to have me already rattled. But when my assistant Yolanda appeared out of nowhere, holding a bowl of popcorn, I will admit to jumping.

The shriek was purely imagined.

"Did you forget something?" Yolanda asked around a mouthful of the salty food. There is something about rock trolls and salts that had her eating the stuff as often as I could get it imported from the mortal realms. I opened my mouth to say something, anything that would explain the situation I was in without making it sound as bad as it was, when Agravane appeared behind me, his breath on the back of my neck the only indication of his presence.

"Would you not do that?" I asked, my voice pitched slightly higher than I was accustomed to hearing. Agravane smirked. He pushed in past me and went to sit on the couch I have in the break area, a room that sounded far less grand than it actually was. One of the perks of working for Death was that I got to play with all the toys, and my break room was full of a very large television, a very comfy couch, and a well-stocked kitchen. I followed Agravane and sat on the couch as well, putting my feet up on the table and pretending to ignore a glowering apparition of Al Capone's standing beside me, still bound but also annoying.

Yolanda followed us in the end sat in the loveseat that was barely big enough for her. "You are both back," she said. "What happened? Did Agravane break someone's nose?"

"Ha ha," Agravane said drily. "Cal didn't invite anyone from the Order of Silence. This is a family reunion. None of Death's family members have offended me, nor have I offended them. So far as I know. No, we are back early because of Cal. He broke guest protocol."

I wondered if the urge to smack Agravane upside the head came from me or from Al, whose bindings were fading now that my active will was lessened. It was distinctly possible that the urge came from both of us. At least Al was staying silent. Yolanda on the other hand, let out a gasp that had her covering her mouth with both her hands and dropping the bowl of popcorn. Great. That would take ages to clean up.

"Cal! How *could* you?" Yolanda said, looking at me as if I had just kicked someone's puppy, or stolen her salt. "Guest protocol is one of the most important laws in Elsewhere. It is the foundation upon which many alliances and dealings have been built. Without guest protocol, many species of Elsewhere wouldn't even speak with one another, for fear of being eaten or destroyed or attacked."

I threw up my hands and leaned my head back on the couch, staring at the ceiling. "Yes. I am fully aware of the problems that came along with this. But I tell you once and for all it was not my fault. Al Capone got control as we were talking with the Taxman and through a stuffed pepper at him. Apparently, the two have some unfinished business."

Agravane snorted. I lifted my head long enough to catch a glimpse of his highly amused expression before setting it back down on the couch. "Well duh. Everyone knows that Capone was arrested for tax evasion rather than the many other things that he did."

"And I wouldn't have had a problem, if some idiots hadn't messed up my taxes. And you know the real kicker," Al said, shaking his finger at me. "When I finally did get those Volstead Act charges put against me, the judge went and said that the tax evasion was the more dastardly, more immediate problem. Of course, those other problems didn't help in my jail time. Plenty of people don't pay taxes. But they *had* to go after *me*."

"Well, naturally. You were a murderer, and you ran illegal booze." After a moment, I realised that I had answered Al and not Agravane or Yolanda. Both of them stared at me, eyes wide. "Ah. Yes, he talks to me. One of the side effects of having temporary possession of his soul."

"That does not sound like a good thing," Yolanda said, a crease forming between her brows.

"Actually, it sounds fascinating. I wonder what it must be like to have someone so charismatic and dangerous inside your head. Though, it sounds as though the side effects were perhaps not worth the price." There was that annoying smirk again, making the urge to smack Agravane upside the head louder than before. This time, I gave into it. Agravane winced and rubbed his head. "Yeah, all right. I get it. Though, I will say that you got off lightly."

Yolanda straightened in her chair, mouth dropping open. "You have already had your punishment sentence? For breaking guest protocol, those can last weeks at a time. Deliberations and counterarguments, ancient treaties and—"

I held up my hand and she felt silent. "It's a fairly simple exchange. As retribution, I am loaned out to the Taxman to see about retrieving a certain amount of back taxes from a fetch based in Chicago."

Agravane blinked. Yolanda blinked. The two of them exchanged glances. They both looked at me. And none of them said anything. I narrowed my eyes behind my glasses. "Okay, what aren't you telling me."

"I'm sure it's nothing," Yolanda said slowly. Agravane shook his head, at least trying to keep the cheeky smile off his face.

"Fetches aren't much of a problem for someone who works for Death. But, I know of only one fetch who lives in Chicago. And he runs the mob."

Later, I would have to ask Agravane why it was that he knew about organised crime in the mortal realms. Or maybe it was fetches that he knew about. Things to do with Death. That would make sense considering he was an employee of mine, and I worked directly for Death. All of these things would have to be understood at a later date. Because all that my brain managed to process was that I was being sent to go collect taxes from a mobster. In Chicago.

Perhaps there was just some sort of cosmic, universal irony that liked to hang around people who had lost their souls, but having Al Capone inside my head, working for the Taxman, and going off to Chicago to deal with a supernatural mafioso, it was all just a little too much. Even with the emotional disconnect that I was feeling from only having a temporary soul, it just bubbled up. I could barely contain it. A moment later, I had thrown my head back and was laughing. Loudly.

TAX HIKE

*I*n Elsewhere, when someone says first thing in the morning, they literally mean first thing in the morning. Agravane and I trudged to the end of Death's lands just as dawn was starting to fill the sky. Agravane had convinced me that bringing him along would be a good idea. I didn't know if the Taxman would approve of my subcontracting my reparation, but considering how little I knew about the supernatural world in Chicago, and how much Agravane really wanted to go, I figured it couldn't hurt. Much. I had offered the possibility to Yolanda, but she took one look at the weather forecast for Chicago—being the middle of summer, it was going to be sweltering—and promptly said no way.

"Did you book a hotel?" Agravane asked.

"A hotel?" I snapped back, quite unhappy at being awake at this early hour and only having had one cup of coffee. "Surely it won't take that long."

"If the Taxman is sending you on a mission to go

acquire the back taxes, then I'd doubt it's going to be a quick snatch and grab. The hotel is necessary." Agravane pulled out his phone and, with a few swipes of his fingers, had apparently booked us into a nice hotel in the middle of Chicago. I wasn't sure what that meant, but considering my brain was still firing on half a cylinder, I let it go.

The two of us came upon the entrance to Death's land, a split in reality where the world turned from silver and grey and blue, to vibrant green. Waiting for us was the Taxman, dressed in almost exactly the same clothes as he had been wearing the day before, minus the stains left behind from the stuffed pepper debacle. He looked at me and Agravane as we approached and frowned.

"This is Agravane," I said, introducing the air elemental with a wave of my hand. "He works for me as a marketing agent at my firm. And has offered his assistance with the more supernatural elements of the situation. Seeing as I'm only human."

The Taxman's frown deepened. "Generally, it is frowned upon to use outside assistance in the repayment of reparations for breaking guest protocol. But, as this does involve elements with which you are unfamiliar, and I am more interested in the completion of the task than seeing you particularly contrite, as you were not in full control, then I will allow this. However, you will have to deliver me the taxes yourself."

I nodded. "I can absolutely do that. And now, is

there a particular passage you would use to get us to the mortal realms?"

I had travelled to the mortal realms in various different ways during my time here in Elsewhere. I had found that Death's transitions were the best, and that many of the others did not go quite so well. Time was one of my least favourite, though I hadn't yet been transported by Life. I imagined that would be something quite worse. The Taxman sniffed as if his very bureaucratic honour had been besmirched. He looked at myself, and Agravane, eyes even lingering half a moment over the spot where Al stood, hands in his pockets and an eager glint in his gaze, before returning to me. He held out his hand, folded his fingers in, and snapped.

Just like that, the world fell away. A moment later, it was back. Only, we were standing in the middle of a very large room with varying many filing cabinets and boxes, papers strewn about, the lights barely lit. I hadn't felt the transition at all, just a mild nudge. Beside me, Agravane sniffed the air and grimaced. That would probably be the smell of musty paper. Or, maybe someone had left a sandwich down here for far too long.

The Taxman took in a deep, cleansing breath and let it out, some of the tension seeming to leave his shoulders. "Welcome to the Chicago branch of the Internal Revenue Service. You will find IDs in the folders there, as well as information on the target and his finances." Agravane and I looked to folders that seemed cleaner and neater than many of the others in the room. At least, they didn't have a layer of dust on them. When we looked back to the Taxman, he was gone.

"Well, all right then. He's not much one for conversation. Now, let's go get checked into the hotel, and then we can see about finding this Dermot Green." Agravane hefted his backpack over his shoulder and walked towards the exit to the storage room with a spring in his step. I started to follow, feeling much less inclined towards the springing.

"Now, I know you ain't much of one to be worried about dying, but your friend isn't so…fortunate. You are going to be dealing with some dangerous people," Al said, walking beside me and looking for more interested in the situation than his casual posture would suggest. He rubbed one hand over the scar on his cheek and then settled it back in his pocket. "And I know you're going to say that you've dealt with dangerous people before. A guy like you has always dealt with dangerous people. But a word of warning, Cal. Magical or otherwise, a crime family is a particular sort of dangerous. You may want to take my advice on some of this."

"Right. And what would the price for that be? A little control of my body? Perhaps another favour? Thank you for the concern, Al, but I shall be doing my best to ignore you from here on out." With that, I shoved past the incorporeal apparition and marched after Agravane.

I hoped it was only my imagination that had a chuckle sounding in the back of my mind.

Now, I really had no idea what day it was the mortal realm, considering that Elsewhere ran on a similar-but-different time stream, but I hadn't expected the office to be busy. As Agravane and I stepped out of the storage room, clipping our ID badges to our shirts, we got some rather unusual stares. These were professional bureaucrats, all people dressed in that sort of business attire that you would expect of the continuous office monkey, their hands full of papers, their fingers poised over keyboards. As one, they all fell silent and watched as Agravane and I walked through the office, passing by them as if it were perfectly normal to have two strangers appear in the middle of the storage room. Given that I was meant to be collecting back taxes from a supernatural entity, I thought it might be wise to explain our presence here.

"We're new in town," I said to a man who looked like he was at least mildly acquainted with computer work, his purple tie was stained with coffee, "on loan from the DC office. You wouldn't happen to know where East Superior Street is?"

I glanced up from the slip of paper where Agravane had written down the hotel address and saw that the man, and several other people who had overheard, were staring at me with open mouths. Had I made some sort of faux pas? Didn't think so, considering that I was human and very familiar with such things as asking for directions and finding a hotel in a busy city. I figured the maybe easy issue was to do with Agravane, whose looks were drawing attention from many of the female, and a few of the male, workers there.

Ignoring the smug feeling from Al in the back of my mind, I coughed pointedly.

"It's about ten minutes drive north of here," the man said. I nodded, thanked him, and then nudged Agravane in the side with my elbow to stop him from flirting with one of the younger workers there. He gave a dramatic sigh and followed after me. I didn't bother stopping anyone else in the office, figuring that my, albeit poor, cover story was sufficiently satisfied. We got a car to take us to the hotel, at which point I started to understand why it was that the man had gaped at me.

"When I told you to book a hotel, I was fairly certain that there would be an understanding of economy involved." I raised my eyebrows pointedly at Agravane, who flashed me a proud grin.

"Indeed there was! I chose the best that this economy has to offer." With that, he strode inside the ridiculously fantastical hotel, of the sort that cost fifteen hundred dollars a night, and offered you every possible thing your heart could desire, except a coupon. I was tempted to whack Agravane over the head, and I did so. Part of me wondered if that was me giving into my lack of soul and the fluctuating emotions that sometimes came with it, or if I was truly annoyed. When Agravane shook off my whack and sauntered up to the desk, checking us in, I was pretty sure that I was truly annoyed.

We were led up to our room by a very pleasant older gentleman who told us all about the city and all the wonderful things that were offered for business and pleasure. Al was listening intently, which meant that half of my mind was processing the words and the other half was wondering just how in the world Agravane expected us to pay for this. I mean, this was all being expensed, but I had never actually discussed with Death what my budget was for such trips. I always thought it was rather assumed that a reasonable budget was to be maintained. Not this bastion of luxury and relaxation.

Then, we were shown our room. It was absolutely marvellous. Having been in Life's over-the-top palace, Death's Old World mansion, and various other castles and places throughout Elsewhere, not to mention a pleasant little hotel in Norway, I can tell you that there is something to be said for ridiculous amounts of luxury. The room was done over in creams and blues, with art on the wall that probably cost a good deal more than the clothes I was wearing. There were, thank goodness, two beds in different suites, each with an attached bathroom and closet where I could stretch my arms out fully. After a perusal of the room, I stumbled back to the smiling older gentleman and placed a large tip in his hand, amazed that I somehow seemed to be able to function even that much with all that was going on. I may be quite fond of such things as designer clothes, a well turned out suit and a perfectly pressed pocket square—though Death had me beat in all aspects in that department—and appreciated to such things as nice kitchens and good offices, but this was on a level I had never quite experienced myself.

Agravane and I waited until the gentleman was

gone before we started thinking about work. "Agravane, have you ever been to the mortal realms?" I tried not to pinched my nose as I said this, instead stuffing my hands in my pockets and staring at the folders the Taxman had given us, resting on a table with a marble top.

"This is my first time. But I have been doing extensive amounts of research as to the appropriate behaviours," Agravane said, smiling eagerly. "This hotel appears to be perfectly in line with what I have seen."

"What exactly do you mean by research?" I was almost afraid to ask where he got the idea of a luxury hotel being normal.

"Yolanda and I have availed ourselves of your video streaming services. You really should be better about your password." If Agravane hadn't been so eager to please, so sure of himself, he would have been endearing. As it was, I spent the next five minutes trying to explain to him that soap operas and television were not accurate representations of reality. He responded with a scowl and a shrug. "Does that mean we will have to move locations?"

I looked around, trying to calculate the cost of each item in my head, trying to figure out just how much trouble I would be in if I allowed us to stay in a fifteen hundred dollar a night hotel room. I wasn't even sure how much money Death had. I knew I got paid a monthly salary, though there was really no need for money considering I didn't really go anywhere and had nothing to buy, but I wasn't quite sure what currency I was paid in. And I wasn't sure what the exchange rate was between that and American dollars.

"Just leave it be," Al said, his incorporeal form running hand over the couch. "Your boss can afford it, trust me. And if he has any problems, you just explain that Agravane was in charge of the hotel booking and didn't do sufficient research. Trust me, Cal. There is something magnificent about living in luxury. About having people at your beck and call, about that power that comes associated with money."

I heaved a sigh, making it as dramatic as possible, before sitting in the chair across from Agravane. "Overestimating money was what got you into prison in the first place, Al. Very well. We can stay. But, if you have any more assumptions about the mortal realm, Agravane, do try to run them by me first or we are going to get into a serious amount of trouble."

Agravane smirked and settled back in the chair. I took a deep breath, this time for real, and held it for a moment. That was all I allowed myself to enjoy such ridiculous amounts of luxury, before settling into do what we had been called here to do. I had violated guest protocol, and if I didn't do what the Taxman was asking, then my further punishment would be much, much worse. I wasn't sure I could handle writing things out in triplicate for a century.

"Dermot Green," I said, flipping open the file. Inside was a picture of a decently interesting looking man, his face full of mischievous character. He was probably about forty-five, with dirty blonde hair that had started going grey, and more lines on his face than one would expect, though given his profession I wasn't terribly surprised. The picture in the file was a candid shot, taken from a telephoto lens—I could recognise such things given my years of experience in dealing with unfortunate media situations for my clients. This one looked as though it had been taken while following the man, caught as he came out of a coffee shop. He didn't look particularly dangerous, but I had met plenty of things that didn't look particularly dangerous. Such was the nature of these magical beings. Yolanda was perhaps the exception, or perhaps the opposite that proves the rule. She looked ferocious and dangerous, and was mildly so, but not compared to many other things. Agravane fits the description perfectly, his immortal good looks and cheeky smile hiding the training that he had been given by a group of assassins: the Order of Silence.

"Says here he owes 1.72 million in back taxes?" Agravane said. "Is that a lot?"

"Depends on how badly they want you," Al said. As Agravane couldn't hear him, I ignored Al's comment and shrugged.

"Honestly, this isn't really my area of expertise. I couldn't tell you if that was a lot or just an average number. I can tell you that Death said he was a fetch. He didn't really explain what that was, except to say that he had once used them as heralds or some such." I looked at Agravane, hoping that he would explain. Most of my googling had come up with articles on how to train your dog and that was not terribly helpful.

Agravane let out a whistle and leaned back in his

chair, tapping his fingers on the table. "Fetch. I haven't dealt with one of them in a long time. They're not terribly widespread as far as beings are concerned. They come from the old Gaelic tradition of Faerie. They are shape shifters, of the sort. The saying is that if you see a doppelgänger of yourself during the morning, then you are going to have a long and prosperous life. If you see them any other time of day, especially in the evening and at night, then you will shortly die. Or so the legend goes. These days, they are just tricksters. Manipulators. It doesn't really surprise me that this one has taken up the life of a crime boss mafioso."

"So, how dangerous are these fetches?" I asked. Not because I was in any particular danger, being unable to die, but I had a very serious aversion to discomfort and pain. Being unable to die meant that I could be tortured, that I could feel pain endlessly and there would be nothing I could do. I had almost been in such a circumstance when I rescued Agravane from the Order of Silence, and then there was that situation with Life back in fourteen ninety-four… I was assured by Doc Graveltoes and others that I had spoken with that in aversion to pain was perfectly normal. Then, I had started to experience the emptiness that having no soul brought on and well, here I was. As messed up as always.

"I'd say they're in not as bad as say, Mercy," Agravane said twirling his hand in the air and creating a small breeze throughout the room. This wouldn't have been anything but showing off if he hadn't been speaking about Mercy, the aurai who had been relatively high up in the Order, the embodiment of mercy and a terrifying assassin. Agravane hated Mercy, for all she stood for, and for the pain that she had caused him. He was also, understandably, terrified of her. "And they're probably slightly worse than your average vampire. Nothing like those royals that you've angered a time or two, but the average one."

"Well, great. But they're Faerie. Don't like iron, telling the truth is compulsive, that sort of thing." My experience with Faerie, the kingdoms and the creatures that claimed the title, was pretty much limited to popular fiction. They didn't tend to encroach on Life's and Death's domains.

"Some things are more true than others," was all that Agravane said. I started rubbing the temples just above my glasses, thinking that it would be about time I got a headache. But, one couldn't have a headache if they were borrowing a soul. There seemed to be limitations to what I could and could not feel. Emotions were fine—especially the emotions that Al Capone was more inclined to feel himself—but physical reactions to emotions seems to be less definitive. As such, I knew that I should have a headache, that I should be feeling some sort of dread in my stomach, but I felt mostly just a mild sense of indigestion, probably from drinking coffee on an empty stomach.

I could not explain how much I longed to be normal again. It went deeper than my lack of soul, or perhaps it was so deep because of it. It was more than just the fact that I worked for Death, it was the fact that being human no longer seemed like my reality. I wasn't sure what I was. But I didn't really fit into the mortal realm anymore, even disregarding the fact that I was in a ridiculously expensive hotel. I wanted something normal to ground my life. My job was far from normal. My friends were a rock troll and an aurai. I wanted a holiday. Or a date with a beautiful woman. Or even just to go and see a concert, watch a game of proper European football.

Instead, I lowered my hand from my forehead, looked back at the file in front of me, and got to work. "So, where do you think our Mr. Green is going to be at this time of day? At home? At work? At a favourite haunt? According to this rather impressive dossier, it seems that he cycles between his home, some sort of microbrewery restaurant thing where he works, or runs his operations, and a coffee shop with a bakery."

Agravane stomach rumbled, and I was suddenly aware of the thought that I should, too, be hungry. "Judging by the sound his stomach is making, I suggest we go find some sort of food. And it's still morning, which means that the coffee shop is the place to be. Trust me, this guy isn't going to be without his comforts. And one of the best comforts and life is having a freshly baked pastry for breakfast." Al nodded definitively.

For once, I agreed with Al. "All right, to the coffee shop then. And try not to buy the whole bakery when we get there. I'd like to at least pretend we had some semblance of self-control."

Agravane rose and stretched, smiling as he did so.

He relaxed into that artistic slouch of his and shrugged. "Don't try to deny it, boss. You like the hotel."

I gave a humpf and stood as well, brushing off my blazer. I didn't say anything, just tucked the folder under my arm and strode from the room. Though, Agravane wasn't wrong. And judging by the smirk I could feel emanating off of Al Capone walking behind me, he too was fully aware that Agravane was not wrong. I tried not to scowl as we trooped into the elevator. At least it was morning. Meeting a fetch in the morning could at least ensure a long life. Whether or not it would be a difficult one was an entirely different matter.

INCOME TAX

Precisely as expected, upon arrival at the coffee shop, Agravane went straight for the counter and its array of, admittedly delicious looking pastries. I headed straight for our person of interest. Dermot Green did not appear to be more prepossessing than his surveillance photo had suggested. He was perhaps slightly less gaunt in person—though that could have been the fact that he had a bear claw stuffed in his mouth—and he looked considerably more stressed. The grey in his dirty blonde hair outnumbered the other strands and the lines around his eyes had absolutely nothing to do with leading a criminal empire instead seeming to come solely from stress. I assumed that this last bit of information was from Al Capone rather than myself, because I had absolutely no idea what it took to lead a mob of supernatural beings, or human ones for that matter. All I knew was that the guy was quaffing coffee and eating pastry like there was no tomorrow.

And then I appeared in front of his table.

A change went over Mr. Green's face, almost like he was becoming another person. His flesh rippled and tried to solidify into something, but it quickly shifted into something else, as if there were two people he was stuck with. Judging by the lack of reaction from the rest of the people in the shop, I gathered no one else could see this.

"Are you okay?" I asked. It would be unfortunate if our target were to expire before I could get the necessary payment from him. Of course, it would also be unfortunate if he were to expire because he was a person and Death was, though a very nice boss, really scary. I wasn't sure about the afterwards bit. Seeing as I couldn't die, I never actually got that far. But Death himself was very powerful. The fetch widened his eyes and slipped back into the face that I had seen in the photos.

"What are you? I can't…It's like there are two of you in one space." I saw fear, or uncertainty at the very least, pass across Mr. Green's face. I decided that it was perhaps better I sit down and explain things. I pulled out the flimsy metal chair across from Dermot and sat down, pushing my glasses up my nose. The air conditioning in the café was working intermittently and I was feeling distinctly warm, given the sweltering summer temperatures outside. I fear this made me look less intimidating than I had hoped. Not that I was a terribly intimidating person, but a guy can hope.

"Ah. Yes. That is rather a long story. It has to do with time travel and my soul and Death. Needless to say, if you're trying to intimidate me by taking on my image, and thereby signalling that I'm about to die, it won't work. For many reasons." I folded my hands on the table and smiled as politely as I could. If I wasn't going to be able to be intimidating, I might as well be polite. The result was less enthusiastic than I would have expected. Dermot Green looked at me skeptically, as if I were a two-year-old telling him I had access to the underworld, then he chuckled. At me.

"What is this? Some sort of ploy to get me to do something stupid? Who do you work for? The drug cartels? Another one of the families?" Dermot shook his head and leaned back in his chair, sipping his coffee as if I were nothing more than a bug swirling around his head. I decided that it was time to break out the big guns, relatively speaking.

I leaned forward, keeping my face deadly calm. "Mr. Dermot Green, I represent the Taxman."

He paused. Considered. And then he scoffed, brows drawn together. He looked at someone behind me and jerked his head upward and some sort of questioning gesture. "Is this guy serious? The Taxman?" He gestured with his hands, waving them about as if I had invoked some ridiculous boogie man that no one feared anymore. I looked behind me over my shoulder and saw Agravane standing with a plate of pastries and coffee. He set the plate down and pushed it towards me, then sat and sipped at his own coffee.

"I would listen to what he has to say, Mr. Green. Cal is on loan to the Taxman until such time as you pay the back taxes. This is a final step taken as the normal tax authorities are not equipped to deal with your particular abilities." Agravane took another sip of his coffee, sounding a whole lot more intimidating than I had managed to do. He looked the part, too, like some sort of well educated fixer or criminal. Sometimes it's hard being average.

"On loan? To the taxman? Who would be stupid enough to lend someone to the taxman?"

Now I was absolutely certain that Mr. Green was not taking us seriously. Either that or he really didn't care about paying his taxes. Not that I blamed him.

"Stupid?" I asked, looking at Agravane and shaking my head. Agravane grinned. "No, Mr. Green. My boss is not stupid. He is powerful, and dangerous. And as the Taxman is his cousin, it seemed only fitting that he assist. And so here I am." I turned my gaze back to Mr. Green, who had the look of someone trying very hard to figure out a puzzle, but without the mental capacity to do it in a timely manner. I decided to help them out. "I work for Death."

This got a reaction. Not the one that I was expecting, but a reaction all the same. Mr. Green leaned back in his chair, set down his coffee, and looked thoroughly relieved. "Death? She, why didn't you say so to begin with? Death is an old friend of the fetches." He even had the gall to smile and pick up the last piece of his bear claw.

"I don't think you understand," I said, pulling off my glasses and cleaning them with a handkerchief. I perched them back on my nose. "Death isn't acting as your friend. He is acting as cousin to the Taxman. Who demands repayment of your taxes, or—"

"Or what? What could the taxman possibly do to me?" Dermot sneered. I looked at the incorporeal figure of Al Capone, standing a few feet away, his hands in his pockets and a mildly interested expression on his face. He shrugged, and tilted his head, the scar on his face showing off to decent effect.

"Ask Al Capone." I picked over the pastries that Agravane had brought, selecting a cherry Danish. "And if prison, of the Elsewhere variety, isn't enough to deter you, then consider this: the Taxman is cousin to Death, who has the authority to make someone leave for a very very long time, experiencing all of the wonders that a clerk to the taxman can experience. Imagine, looking at numbers and filling out form and reading tax law for a hundred years. With no reprieve."

This, out of everything else that had been said thus far, got Mr. Green's attention. He tugged at the collar of his shirt and looked around, as though any of the innocent bystanders and patrons to the coffee shop could possibly help him out of this situation. With a reaction like that, I fully planned on being back in my office by that afternoon—well maybe the next morning. There was no reason to waste such a perfectly good hotel after all.

Then, like some desperate man, he leaned forward conspiratorially, eyes wide, hands ringing together with nerves. "If I pay my taxes, this won't happen?"

"That's all I am here for," I said. "Just to get you to pay the back taxes."

To my surprise, Mr. Green looked even more uncomfortable at this statement. I exchanged a glance with Agravane, who shrugged. I then looked at Al Capone, hoping he could answer some of my questions. He shrugged too.

"See, here's the thing. I've been having problems with my girl. Mathilde. We've been on the outs for a while, on, then off again. But this time seems to be worse than all the others. We've had lawyers screaming at each other for the past six months, and absolutely nothing has been resolved. On account of this... domestic uncomfortableness...a judge decided to freeze all of our assets. Combined and otherwise." Dermot shrugged and looked at me, a little too smug to really be apologetic about the fact that he actually couldn't pay his back taxes because his assets were frozen.

Of course they were. This couldn't be an *easy* trip. If it were, the Taxman wouldn't have bothered asking Death—and therefore me—for help. He would have just waltzed in and made the guy pay himself. Instead, Agravane and I gave each other a look and Agravane nodded.

"I'll go make a call to the hotel and tell them that we shall be here for rather longer than anticipated," Agravane said. He pushed back from the table and strode out of the café, pulling his phone out of his pocket. I turned back to Dermot and tried to remain calm. In the back of my mind, I could feel Al laughing. He sat in Agravane's vacated chair, not that Dermot could see him, but I found it increasingly distracting considering that he was grinning victoriously and laughing.

"Surely there must be something that can be done to get access to the accounts for purpose of paying taxes," I said, expecting absolutely nothing of the sort. My experience has been that when one thing goes wrong, there is not likely to be an easy solution. Life just had things against me that I couldn't overcome, and—I presumed—liked to make things is difficult for me as possible.

"You could file an injunction with the judge, but that would have to go through official channels, and seeing as you work for Death...Also it takes several months to get such things sorted out, and I don't have that sort of time." Dermot looked around anxiously, as if he expected someone to jump out of the shadows and shoot him at any moment. I was fairly certain that he wasn't one of the immortal magical creatures that I had met, but of the more killable variety. Yolanda was like this, and was so was Agravane, though he had the grace and airs of an immortal magical being. I wasn't actually sure whether that was a trait inherent to the aurai, or if his time at the Order of Silence had made him more invulnerable to things like ageing. Again, another area that I hadn't bothered to study, given the fact that my own situation was rather unique.

"Are you afraid that someone is going to kill you?" I asked. I suppose I should have been more concerned, should have been wondering if I was going to get caught in the crossfire, but seeing as I was immune to Death, I wasn't terribly concerned about looking over my shoulder. I certainly wasn't going to look for a killer interested in someone else, no matter how callous that might be. I had a feeling that sort of ruthlessness came more from my proximity to Al Capone's soul and lack of my own. After all, I had spent time without a soul and experienced more things along the lines of volatile emotions and then emotionlessness once the initial stages have worn off. True psychopathy was not really in my wheelhouse.

I glared at Al. He shrugged.

"If I die, all my assets get unfrozen and are willed to Mathilde, and you can easily claim your taxes from her. If that's your concern. No, I don't think someone is trying to kill me…Not just yet at least." At this point, Dermot leaned forward and looked around, this time as if he were expecting someone to overhear. I leaned forward as well, so I could catch his whisper. "You see, by Saturday, I will have signed a deal with the feds. I'm giving up the life, and I'm turning over all of my information to the federal authorities in exchange for entrance into witness protection."

Witness Protection.

Great.

I hadn't had much—or really any—experience with the program, but I knew enough to know that all the assets would be abandoned, or frozen forever or seized or whatever and getting access to them to pay the Taxman would be almost impossible. I mean, presumably, they would take out any amount that was owed to the government to end other people before sealing off whatever assets, but I wasn't entirely sure on that. And even if that were the case, this was the Taxman, not your average IRS. This was something completely different. And if Dermot disappeared, I would have failed. And it would be me having to fill out paperwork for the next century instead of our fetch mobster.

"Ah. And now, why would a smart man like you want to do something so…permanent?" I asked through gritted teeth, the words feeling more like Al's than my own, but welcome enough in exchange for the awkward silence. Because normal Cal had no idea what to do with this.

"It's my second in command, you see. He wants to take over when I retire. But I know him. He's…incompetent. And at the first sign of trouble, our competitors are going to swoop in and try to claim everything, and what a waste. Not to mention that at the first sign of trouble, I will be the first person my lieutenant calls. I will never be able to retire. And I want to retire. Someplace nice and quiet and tropical. Where I'm not trying to suss out empires and worry about backstabbing, literally and figuratively. Surely a guy like you, someone who understands the darker side of things, knows what I mean." Dermot stared at me, as if waiting for response to a question that I desperately hoped was rhetorical. I knew exactly what he meant. I hadn't had a holiday since I began this whole working for Death thing. I had been killed several times, had dealt with murder, had argued with Life, had fought Justice, and that was just in my first week. I knew precisely what he meant. And I also thought he was crazy for having gotten into the situation in the first place.

"Okay. What you want to do with your life is absolutely none of my business." I put down my empty coffee mug and tried not to rub my eyes to relieve some of the headache I knew I should have had. "What is my business is the fact that you still owe back taxes. Your accounts are frozen, so we need to get them unfrozen. Tell me how to do that."

"In four days?" Dermot whistled and shook his head. "The only way I have been told to get my accounts unfrozen is to either divorce Mathilde or to get back together and stop this arguing. You have four days to figure that out, and then I'm vanishing."

"A divorce would be the simplest option." I caught sight of his expression and winced. "Divorce is not the simplest option, is it?"

"Not even a little bit. We've been hashing out divorce papers since this whole thing began. None of us can agree on anything. My lawyer has drawn up a set a couple of days ago, but we haven't had time to get together with her lawyers to go over it." Judging by the smirk that was starting to creep onto his features, I began to have the sneaking suspicion that Dermot was enjoying this. I hastened to remind him why he shouldn't.

"Do you honestly think that the Taxman, the Elsewhere Taxman, won't be able to find you if you're in human witness protection? It doesn't matter where you hide, your fate belongs to him one way or another. Pay him, or work for him." I tried to make my voice more menacing and it came out rather a lot more intimidating than I had thought. I glanced wide-eyed over it at Al, who gave me a shrug and then chuckled as he looked at the table. Great, one more thing to worry about. He was finding his way out of the cage that I had put him in. I was either going to have to do some serious meditation soon, or arrange a deal with him. Given my new four day deadline, I didn't really have time for an evening wasted on meditating to put the criminal back in his cage.

Thank goodness, one of the two criminals at the table was listening to me. Dermot had gone all blotchy, either from anger or fear. I raised my brows expectantly. "Okay, okay. If you can get Mathilde to actually agree to sit down with me, to go on a date or whatever, that I'll try my best to patch things up with her."

"Perfect." I pushed back from the table and tugged at the edges of my blazer, straightening the lines. "Shall we go back to your apartment so that we might prepare a plan of action? I am going to need rather a lot more detail on your situation with your estranged wife, or I am never going to be able to get the two of you in a room together, let alone make it a date."

With a reluctant nod, Dermot agreed. He rose from the table and heaved a sigh at my gesture for him to lead the way. I had a feeling this was going to be rather complicated. And I had once done relationship counselling for Life and Death, so I knew complicated. Agravane was waiting for us outside the café, an eager smile telling me that he had extended our stay at the obscenely expensive hotel for a while. I really hoped Death didn't mind us expensing this. Or I was going to have to repay him after I finished repaying the Taxman.

"We're going to help Dermot get back together with his wife in the next four days, so that he can give us access to the accounts and we can get our taxes," I said Agravane. Understandably, the aurai's mouth dropped open, making him look not so much like a gaping fish as a very well proportioned depiction of surprise. My scowl started creeping up again. I shoved it down, and instead frowned at the sweltering weather that started beating down on us as we walked across the sidewalk.

I was trying to figure out ways to woo a woman—something I hadn't done since before hiring on with Death—when I was suddenly aware of the sensation of being flattened. My head cracked down into my spine, which collapsed like an accordion until my legs again about beneath me. Given the flash of unseeing whiteness I saw for a brief second, I assumed that I had just been killed. You might be thinking that I was a bit cavalier at this, but given how much it had happened in recent times, the only part I really disliked was the whole pain bit. But I healed from every fatal injury, whole and well enough to survive another day. It really was quite depressing.

When I came to, a large chunk of smashed wood, wire and metal bits was being hauled off of me. I felt my shirt sticky with blood, though the wounds that had produced the liquid would soon be sealed over. My glasses, though, had a crack across one lens.

I felt the tragedy of the last couple of days creeping up on me. I just felt so overwhelmed. All I wanted to do was my job, and here I was, dealing with the Taxman, trying to convince a criminal to get back together with his wife, and I had been just killed by a piano falling from the sky.

I was certain there was no way that things could get worse, even if I was tempting the Universe by even thinking it. There was just no way.

Once the majority of the piano had been pulled off me, I rolled onto my back and let out a groan. Just because I healed from the fatal injuries didn't mean that they didn't hurt. I was really sore, and I doubted my back would ever be quite the same. I shielded my eyes against the sun.

"You are not dead," a female voice said, musical and highly appealing in my moment of agony. I squinted up at the silhouette above me, seeing a flash of black and a flash of white surrounding a feminine figure. "You should be dead."

I leaned up on my elbows and blinked a few times, trying to get a better look at her through my one cracked glasses lens and the one that was whole, but very dirty. What I saw made everything that I had been through in the last two days completely worthwhile. She was relatively short, but built as though she could fight her way through an army and do so with grace and style. She wore some sort of black tactical jump-suit, a tank top cut revealing well proportioned arms and a beautiful complexion in a dark colour, almost a blue-grey. Her hair was pure white, flowing down to her waist, though she couldn't have been older than me, and I was in my prime. She scowled down at me, her expression of disapproval even more capable than my own.

"Wish magic never fails. Why are you not dead?"

I had no idea what she was, I had no idea who she was, I had no idea why in the world she was trying to kill me, though I realised it could have just as easily been Dermot that she was after, but I knew one thing very clearly. She was the most beautiful creature I'd ever seen. And she wanted me dead.

TAX REFUND

The piano movers ended up calling an ambulance, fawning over me until the paramedics arrived. It was rather complicated to explain to the paramedics that no, the piano had not actually killed me, because it hadn't really fallen on me. The blood was from a scraped knee, though I don't think they bought that much. In the end, I was sent away with chagrined looks and promises to the piano movers that I would not press charges or sue them more anything for accidentally dropping a piano in my near vicinity.

Afterwards, though, when the mortal humans had stopped staring at me and the wreckage of the piano, and I was left with Dermot Green, Agravane, and this mysterious newcomer, we all decided that perhaps it would be best to get off the street and had to somewhere a bit more private. Even considering that this incredibly dangerous, angry, beautiful woman had tried to kill me, I was inclined to let her come along.

After all, she couldn't actually do that much damage to me. I mean, she could. She could hurt me quite a lot, but I didn't think that was her intent. Or maybe I just desperately hoped so. I had no useful advice from Al on that part, either. He seemed to be still taking in the shock of having experienced death without actually dying. He seemed uncharacteristically quiet, his eyes darting about as if expecting a threat to jump out from any corner.

We went to Dermot's apartment. It was the only place that we could think to go. No one would be listening there and it would be a good place to set up a base of operations. Dermot let us inside and I had a moment to goggle at the sheer opulence of the place. It was, if possible, even more posh than the hotel. The furniture seemed custom; the table in the centre of the kitchen was made of a single massive slab of live edge wood with metal legs. The art on the walls was expensive and modern and made absolutely no sense to me. But I hadn't been a high end marketing agent for nothing. I recognised the quality of his wine collection, the impeccable cleanliness behind his living room. And when I sank into the leather couch, I recognised that it was a very good one by the way it tried to eat me.

Dermot closed the door after everyone was inside, and locked it conspicuously behind us. Our tentative silence broke.

"What are you, some sort of demon?" the woman asked. She folded her arms and glared down at me, standing before me and taking me end as though I were not only a threat but an annoying one.

"Yeah, no. That's not how this works. You were the one who tried to kill me. I want some answers," I said. She glowered at me and said nothing. I took a breath and went to wipe my glasses on my shirt, only to realise that my shirt was kind of covered in blood and guts. Not to mention, cleaning wouldn't do anything about the massive crack across my lens.

"Dermot and I will go will search for some clothes for you, Cal. We'll let you sort everything out." With that, Agravane turned on his heel and marched to grab Dermot by the elbow, leading him into some back part of the apartment. Dermot protested, but acquiesced in the end.

"Look, I'm not going to attack you. You are welcome to sit on the couch. Actually, I would prefer it, if only to make you stop staring down at me. You are a guest here in Mr. Green's apartment. You would do well to remember that." Finally, I said something that seemed to hit this woman. She huffed, tossed a lock of hair over her shoulder and sat in the couch across from me.

"I am only cooperating because of guest protocol." She folded her arms and leaned back.

"I don't care. I just want to understand. How about we start with your name? I'm Cal Thorpe." I put a hand on my chest and winced as it came a sticky. I was going to need a shower.

The woman took in a deep breath, her blue-grey skin darkening ever so slightly. She let the breath out in a huff and groaned. "I am Neja. A djinn."

Okay that one was new to me. I mean, I had a

general idea, but she didn't look like some sort of genie, and I definitely didn't see any magical containment vessels nearby. "A djinn? That's not like…"

Neja's a scowl deepened before she sighed and gave in. She leaned forward and propped an elbow on her knee, resting her chin in her hand. "You are an unusual being, Cal Thorpe. You do not have the magical signature of a wizard, and you appear to be human. You are in the company of an aurai and a fetch. Yet you do not know what a djinn is."

I leaned forward and copied her position, resting my arms on my knees and trying not to look as weary as I suddenly felt. Weary and curious. "Yeah. It's complicated. I'll tell you what, you explain to me why exactly you want me dead and I will explain to you precisely where I fit in the grand scheme of things, as far as I'm aware. And then, perhaps we can both go about our day."

Neja considered, eyes darting to the doors in the window as if she expected someone else to appear, or if you were looking for an escape route. She nodded. "A djinn is the basis of your human genie stories. We are spirits, born of smoke and ash and fire. Those of us born under a dark moon seek the power to control. Those of us born under the full moon are considered generally benevolent. Those of us born any other time run the gamut. I was born under a wolf moon as it started to wane. Djinns holds the province of wish magic. There are many, hmm, *rules* for approaching a djinn about a wish, and even more rules for actually applying the wish. It is unpredictable magic, which is why I don't rely on it for my job."

I nodded, following so far. Though, her imprecise statement about what moon she was born under was not terribly encouraging. "And your job is?"

Neja straightened and lifted her chin with a proud smile, looking for all the world like a young woman who had accomplished a great deal while others told her that she would not. "I am a bounty hunter and private investigator."

I coughed. "What?" I squeaked. I coughed again and repeated the question, this time in not quite so squeaky a voice.

"I enjoy it. And I'm good at it. No client has ever been able to escape me, nor do they fault my investigative skills. But with you, I encountered a problem. See, I was approached by a banshee who knew the proper rituals to engage me in a wish exchange. Dangerous, but she seemed to know the price. She pointed at you as you were exiting the coffee shop and wished you dead. I obliged." Neja narrowed her eyes at me, interest flickering in their silvery depths. "You did not oblige."

Al finally piped up, leaning in close to my ear and expressing his nervousness. "Look here. I'm all for facing danger head on, but there's something not quite right with this one. Don't go giving away your secrets, Cal."

I considered sparing him a glare, but I decided just to ignore him instead. "Yes, well, there isn't anything I can do about that. See, I work for Death. And in the course of performing my various assignments, Death lost my soul."

Neja's eyes brightened even more and she seemed extremely interested, then she seemed to understand precisely what it was that I was saying and she scowled fiercely, as though I had just killed her cat. "You cannot die."

I shrugged. "Nope."

"I still have to fulfil the wish." Neja frowned. "Unless the wish is rescinded, then I have no choice but to continue attempting to fulfil it."

"You what?" Don't get me wrong, it was a little disconcerting to hear that someone wanted me dead in the first place. I mean, I hadn't even been in the mortal realm for a full day. But Neja seemed like a decent enough sort, as far as super dangerous and scarily beautiful bounty hunter djinns went, and since she couldn't actually kill me, then I figured we would just call it good. But if she still had to fulfil the wish, then we were going to have some problems. "You mean, you're going to attempt to kill me again?"

Neja shrugged and stretched. "Again and again and again, until either the wish is rescinded, you go back to Elsewhere, or you die."

I looked around uncomfortably and felt my palms start to sweat, which really was not very pleasant considering they were covered with all sorts of...gore. "There really aren't any other options, are there?"

"Unfortunately not. Wish magic is very specific." Neja stretched and laid back on the couch, kicking off her shoes and looking for all the world like she was perfectly content to live there and take a nap even after announcing that she was going to do her very best to kill me. Instead she would only achieve the goal of causing me great deals of pain. "Don't look so nervous, Cal. I can't do anything here. I'm under guest protocol. But once you step out of the apartment, or I step out of the apartment, then, well, things will change. I wouldn't worry about it too much, considering you can't die. What's the worst that could happen?"

I looked down at my hands, wondering if perhaps Al was right. This djinn was beautiful, and confident and capable, but she was still extremely dangerous and she had one goal in mind. I didn't want to tell her that what she could do to me would amount to my worst nightmare. To live endlessly in pain. "You know, Neja, you're right. What's the worst that could happen? Now, if you don't mind, I'm going to go take a shower and change into something less violent. My assistant, Agravane will keep you company and maybe we can figure out a way to talk to your client and rescind the wish magic."

Neja stretched and put her arms under her head, tangling her fingers in her white hair. She watched me as I stood and shuffled awkwardly back to where Agravane and remote were hiding. "What exactly is an agent of Death doing in Chicago?"

"Ah. Yes. I'm on loan to the Taxman until such time as I can get Mr. Green, the fetch, to pay his back taxes…things are a little complicated, as his finances are tied up in a legal battle with his…" I turned and stared down at Neja who calmly looked back at me, unconcerned. I noticed her trousers riding up on her ankle and saw a knife strapped there. I swallowed. "His wife. A banshee. She wouldn't happen to be the same banshee who hired you, would she?"

Neja shrugged. "I don't know. What was her name?"

"Mathilde," Dermot said, appearing from the hallway where apparently, he had been eavesdropping. I didn't begrudge him, it wasn't every day that one dealt with such strange occurrences before lunch. Even if you were a member of the magical community. "Mathilde Anne Green."

Neja had tilted her head and nodded, settling in deeper to her relaxed position. "Yes. That was her."

I winced and turned to derma. "I think your wife might have directed her wish magic at the wrong person. I think she meant to kill you."

To my surprise, the fetch simply smiled and even blushed a little. "She still cares."

Oh, yeah. It was definitely going to be one of those weird jobs. I clapped Dermot on the shoulder, not feeling remotely bad about leaving a smear of dirt there. His wife had pointed at the wrong person and had resigned me to a fate of extreme pain. This was better than Dermot's death, I supposed, considering my circumstances with the Taxman, but it sure didn't make me feel any better. And it made things even more complicated, because now it would have to deal with a djinn looking over my shoulder with various weapons, and had to figure out how to reconcile Dermot with a wife who wanted him dead. Date night was going to be fun. So. Very. Fun.

—

Agravane stood in the door as I finished buttoning my borrowed shirt, the sleeves too long and the fabric too shiny. It was better than my ability torn garments. "This is exactly like television, Cal. I mean, we have to get back taxes by means of helping someone solve the relationship, meanwhile someone has mistakenly put a target on your back instead of our client and we still have to do everything by Saturday. Yolanda was right. The mortal realms are very fun."

"I wouldn't call this fun," I said, fixing my glasses on my nose. "This is going to get very dangerous. We now have to protect Dermot from his wife accidentally making more threats against him. Not to mention the fact that he is, oh I don't know, giving up his entire mob operation to the authorities. His people are not going to like that. Besides, having to deal with being killed periodically is going to make enacting our plans extremely slow."

"So you're just going to let her kill you over and over and over again until this job is done?" Agravane folded his arms and leaned against the doorframe, preventing me from getting out. "I know that you are not magically inclined. You are human, and thereby weak in comparison to pretty much everything that roams Elsewhere, but you can at least *try* to defend yourself. You would perhaps do well if people considered you dangerous enough not to bother with. And if I'm constantly having to fight off paramedics and clean up your clothes and everything else, then you are not going to be much help and we are never going to get these taxes. You will be lost to the Taxman for a century."

Agravane had a point. Generally speaking, my position as marketing and public relations agent to Death should have been enough protection to keep me from most every harm, except in retaliation to those things that I caused myself. The problem was, that I was getting involved with the things that weren't at all bothered by my position in Elsewhere, and still sought to do me harm or have me dead. Defending myself against such things, on the other hand, was an entirely different matter.

Humans were numerous, oblivious, and at the bottom of the food chain in Elsewhere. In the mortal realms, they were considered prey, but dangerous prey. Simply because of sheer control and numbers and a certain je ne sais quoi that the magical beings hadn't figured out how to counteract. However, humans did have a few things that most creatures in Elsewhere did not. A fierce desire to live and a disregard for many of the old traditions had made them less incapable than otherwise. The fact of the matter still stood, though, that as far as humans were concerned I was pretty nonthreatening. I was not athletically inclined except for your daily run and the occasional hefting of ten or twelve bags of groceries up the stairs. I had no skill for magic, though Yolanda had tried to teach me. Not that she had any skill for magic. And the one massive sword fight I had gone in was mostly

playacting for the sake of onlookers so that my opponent and I could figure out a plan to, well, save the
world.

All things considered, I really needed to improve
my skills. "I'm not sure that trying to develop the ability
to defend myself while fighting off a djinn whose wish
magic has been directed to kill me is a great idea."

Agravane nodded, his frown serious. Al, on the
other hand, clapped me on the shoulder and grinned
broadly. "No, this is in the perfect time to get you in
shape. How do you think I came to have so much
power? I didn't just wait until things were all nice and
quiet and then decide to train then, to gather political
power then, to control the booze trade then. I had to
struggle through adversity, moving my way up the
ranks with people doing their very best to cause me
harm. How do you think I dealt with the Untouchables
for so long? I was on top of the world, and it was not
because I waited to try and improve my
circumstances."

I gave Al a weak smile. Agravane sensed my silence
and raised his brows expectantly. "Perhaps I should
work on these skills sooner rather than later."

Agravane nodded and clapped his hands together,
decision made. He turned from the door so I could pass
and go deal with our mobster and the djinn, then slung
his arm around my shoulder and grinned ferociously.
"Don't worry, Cal, I learned enough fighting techniques
from my time in the Order of Silence to be able to you
whip you into shape in no time. From now on, every
evening and every morning, we shall put you through

training drills. That djinn won't catch you unawares for too much longer."

That same djinn appeared in front of me almost as soon as we entered the kitchen, holding a cup of coffee and twirling a knife in her hand. Agravane surged forward and did his best to knock the weapon from her hand, but she skipped back with light step, keeping hold of the knife and not spilling a single drop of coffee as she evaded the aurai's attack. "Ah ah, you mustn't do that. Guest protocol is in place, after all. Our host has allowed me to stay for the deliberations seeing that my client seems to have mistaken her target. Though there is nothing I can do about that, as wish magic has already been enacted and released. However, I can put an end to this."

" Why would you help us?" Agravane growled. I rolled my eyes and shuffled my way into the kitchen, going for the pot of coffee. It was barely lunchtime, but I already felt as though the morning and drained away all the energy I had gotten from my first dose of caffeine. Dying and being brought back was rather hard on a body.

"Relax, aurai. Do you think that I want to spend the rest of my days following Cal around and trying to kill him when he cannot be killed? I mean, there are many ways to do such a thing, but it would get dull after a while. And besides, I don't typically like to kill people. In this instance, Mathilde knew about enacting wish magic and there was nothing I could do." Neja held her coffee close to her and tried to look primly at Agravane. She seemed more uncertain than annoyed. Or at least, that was how she appeared.

"All right, the pair of you. Let's just try to work together for now. Guest protocol is in place until one or both of us leaves the apartment. For now, I need to know everything you can tell me about your wife, Dermot. What does she like to eat, what are her favourite colours, are there any activities that you have promised her you would do in the last two years that you haven't done? I don't care how embarrassing you find any of this, I need to know. Your wife has escalated matters by trying to kill you. If you want to win her back, then I need a place to start." I sipped my coffee and glared at the mobster. He held up his hands and shrugged. He gestured to the table where Agravane had already set up a laptop. I stopped before the computer and try not to dwell on the complicated nature of my task.

"You're kinda grumpy, Cal," Neja said, sitting across from me. She tilted her head and blinked at me, the motion in human and yet purely female. I fought not to fidget. "Perhaps your aurai friend is right and you do need to learn how to better you defend yourself. Then the world could not take you quite so by surprise."

I coughed and tried to hide the cost by my coffee. It didn't work. "Defence has never been my strong suit. And I'm only grumpy because I was up early this morning to travel from Elsewhere. I'm a marketing agent. I don't normally get involved in relationship advice."

Agravane slid into the chair beside me, smirking.

"And what about that whole situation between Life and Death? I believe you had to travel back to the fifteenth century in order to get that sorted out."

Neja laughed, the sound infectious, like a chime. "You did what?"

I think into my chair, fighting the flush that came up and failing miserably. "How about we just deal with the situation at hand?"

"By all means," Dermot said. "I have no intention of being bound to the Taxman."

"Okay. Let's talk dinner. Dermot do you think that you can get Mathilde to agree to meet you at a restaurant or something? Without lawyers. Lawyers tend to kill the romantic mood." I started pulling up a list of über fancy restaurants in Chicago, thinking that maybe a show of affection by way of spending extravagantly was perhaps in order. Granted, Dermot's finances were sealed, so he didn't really have money besides pocket change to spend. That meant that I was going to have to put this on my account. After Agravane's mixup with the hotel, I wasn't quite sure how Death would feel about an extravagant spending session in the name of winning over a banshee to unlock funds to help Taxman. Alternatives, though, were limited.

"I think I can get her there," Dermot said. He straightened his shoulders and lifted his chin. "I'll just woo her over the phone. She can't resist me that way."

Well that would be useful. I handed Dermot my phone and he dialled. He put the phone on speaker so that all of us could hear, then cleared his throat, put on a charming smile—which benefited no one, but apparently helped his confidence—and waited for her to answer the phone.

"Hello? This better not be a spam call." Mathilde's voice was sharp, impatient. She sounded at once older and more feminine than I had expected, though I wasn't really sure what to expect from a banshee. Screaming perhaps.

"Hello Mathilde. This is no spam call." Dermot started, which wasn't a terrible start. Neja winced, which informed me that perhaps it was a terrible start. My experience with women had mostly involved dating other agents from the company, or the occasional nice girl I met at a coffee shop. The longest relationship I'd had lasted nearly a year, though it ended with my stuff being thrown out of the building, so I wasn't quite sure I could call that a success. Neja, apparently, was right. Mathilde's response was not pleasant.

"What are you doing call me, you stupid fetch? I told you that if you ever tried to contact me without our lawyers present that I would put your head in a blender. You're a womaniser, Dermot. And you seem to think that you can have things your own way without facing any of the consequences." There was that extra shrill voice that I was expecting from the banshee. I scratched my ears, trying to with this the impulse to block out the noise entirely.

"Mathilde, that's not—" Dermot's eyes were wide and he didn't seem to be having the upper edge.

"I don't care what sort of scheme you've got up your sleeve now. You were charming once, but I've grown wise. Enjoy your last days, you rat." There was a distinctive click on the other end of the line and a shrouding silence that followed.

It was Neja who broke the silence, giggling and trying to contain her laughter behind her hand. She gave up and leaned back, letting out a full belly laugh.

"I see why she used wish magic to try and kill you," Neja said, wiping a tear from her eye. Dermot frowned, glaring the hole into the table. His features shifted to become closer to hers, his anger trying to show through and forewarned of her death or some such fetch magic. I was not actually sure how it worked, but it didn't seem to stick with Neja. "Relax. She's obviously angry. You just have to figure out what you did, apologise, and invite her to dinner."

Dermot glared harder at the table. "I didn't do a single thing. She's the one with mental problems. She's the one who needs to apologise for treating me like this."

I swallowed nervously and exchanged a glance of Agravane, who was looking amused, though not quite as amused as Neja. "This is going to be more complicated than I thought," I said.

"It's exactly like the television!" Agravane grinned. "Just wait till I tell Yolanda."

JOINT TAX RETURN

Since Dermot was basically completely useless and trying to figure out how to win back his not quite ex, I sent him to go take a shower and get primped up for the inevitable disaster that was going to be his date night. That left Neja and Agravane and I to sort out these problems. The first bit would require getting Mathilde to actually listen to us, to show up at the restaurant and stay there long enough to have a proper date night.

I was going to need some help.

"Neja," I said warily, watching her stretch back in the chair as if she owned it. "Say I need to find out some information on Mathilde. Could you do that for me?"

She considered, running her hands through her hair. She straightened, smirked, nodded. "My rate is five hundred a day plus expenses and bonus for any unusual activities."

I spluttered. "Five hundred a day?! Aren't...I mean... I can't just...But...How?"

"You may want to explain to your boss the nature of being a supernatural PI and bounty hunter. Or perhaps she explained to him the concept of money. He seems to be having a hard time." Neja tilted her head and smiled Agravane who returned the smile with one of his standard butter wouldn't melt grins.

"Cal is holding on to some of the strange human notions that he has. But he is very clever and good at his job." Agravane patted me on the head, which was not at all patronising. Sometimes, I really hated being the only ordinary human amongst the world of the magical and immortal. Everyone's expectations were too high.

"All right, I'll explain this to you simply. I work for some of the most powerful beings in the known universe. Dragons, vampires, elves, Fae. All of these beings are known for being powerful and they pay well. You work for Death, arguably one of the most influential beings out there. Trust me, Cal, you can afford my rates." Neja leaned forward and fixed me with a grin that showed off her teeth, which I noted were slightly pointed. "And if you can't, then you'll just have to learn to do without."

I frowned. While it would be possible to do this without Neja, the time constraint that had been placed on Agravane and myself, as well as the new difficulties of having what amounted to a bounty on my head, and the fact that Mathilde was the one who put it there, it would be very difficult to do would need to be done. If

I had Neja helping to find information, providing me with assistance when necessary, and frankly if I knew where she was at all times, then things would be much easier. Not only for trying to get out of this mess but also so I would know when the death threats and attempts would be coming. It wasn't quite the defensive strategy that I'm sure Agravane had in mind, but considering training took time and that was the one thing we didn't have, then it would have to do.

"Can I at least get itemised receipts?" I asked, holding my hands together. Neja laughed, squeezing my hands, then settled back in her chair.

"I see why Death hired you. You are most amusing. Now, what exactly do you need me to do?"

"I need you to find out what Mathilde likes and doesn't like. I need to figure out what her favourite place to eat is, what sort of flower she adores, what sort of sparkly baubles get her attention, what exactly our wayward mobster did to make her so angry, and things like that. I need to know everything about her so that I can prepare Dermot to sweep her off her feet. We have a lot to do and not a lot of time to do it. I want them meeting with the lawyers by Friday at the absolute latest." I pulled out my phone and took down some notes, trying to gather my ideas. It was a little out of my depth. While in theory I knew how to woo a woman, I had never dealt with quite this level of soap opera dramatics before. I looked up and saw Neja and Agravane staring at me, mouths slightly open.

"Is he serious?" Neja mouthed to Agravane, not once taking her eyes off of me.

"He's serious." Agravane said, giving me a sympathetic look. "Cal, listen. I know you're trying to go about this the best way you know how, but the magical community does not do romance quite like the human community."

I stifled the urge to roll my eyes. Human females were not different from any other females that I had thus far met. Okay, yes, many of the magical beings that I had met were extremely powerful, could probably tear me apart with their bare hands, but they were still fundamentally female. "The rules of Elsewhere trade on power, do they not?"

Neja furrowed her brows into a thoughtful expression and nodded. She looked a little like a fox trying to understand an owl.

"In order for Mathilde to find Dermot appealing once more, he not only has to make up for past mistakes, usually in involved in the payment of a reparation of some sort, or a favour. owed, or a public apology of some sort, but he has to charm her into staying with him—at least long enough to sign the stupid papers. That requires a display of power does it not?"

Neja propped her head in her hand and appraised me once more, this time looking a little more wolfish. "Perhaps you understand more than you look like you do."

I hesitated; was that meant to be a compliment? I fidgeted with my phone and eventually set it down on the table, locking the screen. "In any case, since Mathilde and Dermot live here permanently in the mortal realm, then their measure of power is going to be synonymous with that of humans. At least, closer in meaning. Therefore, an apology on bended knee in the middle of a restaurant with a display of power—that is the ability to provide wealth ostentatiously without fear of reparation from potential threats—is a good place to start."

"Well, you're not entirely wrong. There is certainly, usually, a good deal more manipulation involved, pitting intelligence against brute force and the such, but you have the fundamentals down," Neja said. I smiled weakly.

"The problem is that we have a very limited amount of time. So if you wouldn't mind perhaps going and finding out this information, that would be very useful." I tried to sound pleasant, polite even, but I fear that I failed in the midst of my growing anxiety that I would be stuck signing tax documents for the rest of my life—or at least the next century of it. Without a soul, theoretically I would live forever. But that was too depressing to think about just then, so I decided not to. I looked down at my hands again. "Look, I know that you don't know me and that I don't know you, but I need all the allies I can get right now. So I'm going to take a chance and trust that you are to be held at your word. I'm hiring you Neja."

"Oh I believe that you need all the help you can get." Neja laughed and then held out her hand for me to shake. I took it, not entirely sure where this would get me, and was surprised at the warm tingling sensation that ran up my arm. When she pulled away, I looked at my hand, wondering if some sort of magic had been enacted there. Instead, there was nothing. Maybe it just couldn't be seen. I lowered my hand and nodded.

"Thank you." I turned back to my phone and the impromptu to do list that I had started there. Neja stood, winked at me, headed out the door.

"Oh and Cal," she tossed over her shoulder, eyes sparking, "don't think that being my client doesn't mean that I won't try to kill you."

With that, she was gone.

"Well, well," Agravane said, folding his arms and leaning back in his chair. He kicked his feet up and rested them on the table. "A djinn. Not every day that you can catch the eye of a djinn. Well done, Cal."

"What are you…No, it's not like that," I tried to protest. Agravane shrugged and lifted his hands in surrender. His smirk remained.

"Whatever you say, boss. When all of this is done, we'll see. Yolanda was convinced that one of the vampires would fall in love with you. I rather thought that you were too grumpy to let something like that happen. You needed at least a decade of tempering. I would say more, but immortality is relatively new to you and I think you still think in terms of a different time frame than most of us."

"Should I be disturbed that you and Yolanda have enough free time to discuss my love life, or lack there-of?" I asked pointedly. "I'm sure I can find some more work for the two of you to do."

"We talk about it purely during our own free time. Now, I know what Neja is going to do, but what am I going to do? For that matter, what are you going to do?" I allowed Agravane's obvious change of subject sense because I didn't really want to talk about any of this at the moment. Yes, I found Neja interesting. She intrigued me. And she was very beautiful. But so were many other magical beings, immortal or otherwise. There was something about the extra vitality that magic gave them. We had other matters to think of.

"I am going to go directly to Mathilde and beg for her to meet Dermot tonight. You are going to stay here and make sure that he is ready for tonight. That means you have to school him on how to treat Mathilde, how to get on her good side. If she has one."

"I'll do my best. I've never had this sort of problem, so it's going to take some investigation to figure out how to solve Dermot Green." Was that arrogance talking or just the confidence that what he said was true? I could never quite figure that out with Agravane. When I had found him, he had been impaled on a stalagmite, and was doing his very best to reconcile his naturally argumentative and perhaps insubordinate tendencies with the rigid requirements of balance that were demanded by the Order. Since he'd started work for me, he had become more confident, more willing to ask questions and step outside the boundaries, to argue and poke. He was especially good at getting people to open up, to talk with him, to treat him like one of their best friends. And yet sometimes, I saw a glimmer of doubt, some sort of barrier that he couldn't quite figure out how to overcome. How to relate to other people.

Or maybe that was just me projecting my inadequacies on him. After all, Death knows that I sometimes had problems talking to other beings of Elsewhere. Though, much of that was to do with ignorance of their nature as opposed to otherwise.

"You alright, Cal?" Agravane asked. The question startled me and I found myself staring at him for several moments, not quite comprehending. "It's just, you seem to be taking all of these things that happened the last couple of days rather well. And I don't mean like the emotionless zombie that you were before you got hold of Al Capone soul, I mean you've been accused of violating guest protocol even though you were not the one who threw the pepper—there are well-known circumstances of possession that must be taken to an account—and then there's the whole being loaned to the Taxman. He seems benign, but he holds sway over much of the bureaucracy that runs throughout Else-where. Many of our treaties and records have been overseen by him. There is no one better at winnowing out the truth. And then this whole situation with the mobster, and being crushed by a piano, and now working with Neja...I just think that you don't seem quite as upset as I would have expected."

I leaned back in my chair. Al, whom I hadn't heard from in some time, whispered in my ear. "What does he expect, you'd act like some sort of floundering idiot?"

"As far as I can see it, I have a couple of options. Scream and run in circles, which would accomplish exactly nothing. Go back to Death and try to explain to him that I wasn't in control of my actions. Work for the Taxman for a century. Or I can move forward with this particular problem, taking everything one day at a time and not worrying about everything else that's going to come crashing down on my head in the future—literally or otherwise." I tried to smile and push up my glasses on my nose. They didn't fit quite as well as they used to, not that this particular pair ever seem to fit properly.

"You just don't seem to be quite so…Grumpy." Agravane actively looked concerned, which was interesting.

"Grumpy? You're worried because I'm not grumpy?"

Al snickered and clapped me on the shoulder, which I found extremely annoying considering that he was incorporeal. "This guy's got you pegged."

"You know what, you're right. Let's just deal with the problem at hand and move on. That's all any of us can ever do, right?" Agravane pushed back from the table and went to go check on Dermot, spouting something about appropriate wardrobe or not to use so much aftershave. That left me at the table, wondering what had just happened.

I thought being in the moment, living life day by day, was a good thing. It had taken an excursion back to fourteen ninety-four for me to realise that I actually liked working for Death, that I enjoyed experiencing the magic that this new world had to offer. Okay, yes, much of this new world wanted to kill me at any given time, but there was wonder there, too. I had made friends. They taught me that perhaps embracing the moment was all anyone could ever do. And then I had come back and tell with the aftereffects of losing my soul, and now here I was. The only problem was, I couldn't quite tell if my ability to take things one problem at a time was coming from the notorious criminal that my right shoulder or if it was me. Because it was just challenges, ready for me to overtake them, for me to bury them and climb on their ashes. The more I achieved, the greater I would become.

Okay…That was definitely the mobster talking.

"Al, we need to have a word about your exertion of influence on me." I pushed back from the table and left, though I did take a minute to look over my head in case Neja had left some sort of trap for me as soon as I left the apartment. There didn't seem to be anything, and I was uninjured as I left the building, so I assumed that things were going to be okay for the moment.

"I'm not doing anything that you wouldn't do in my position. Besides, there's bound to be some mingling when our soul resides in your body. Life force and soul feed off of one another, so here we are. Don't get mad, Cal, *embrace* it. Use the power. In my time, everybody loved me. The people praised my name, they thought of me as a public hero. Okay, yes, I had a few fingers in some unsavoury pies, but that only enabled me to lower crime, to snuff out the competition." Al had his hands in his pockets and was walking around like a peacock, taking in the streets of Chicago as though he owned them. I felt the rising anger, not only at myself for not realising his influence earlier but also at him for exerting it, for thinking that he still had a chance in the mortal realm, that I was going to be a willing partici-pant in his schemes. I knew that the amount of anger I was feeling was also proportional to his influence over me, but I didn't really care.

"Al Capone, do not mess with me. I will cage you again, lock you in a box so small and airtight that you will think fondly on your time in prison." I tried to keep my voice down, but I still got a few strange looks from people who were walking by in the sweltering heat. I smoothed my borrowed shirt and tucked my hands into my pockets, moving with confidence.

"You're learning," was all he said. I ignored him and called up a ride on my phone, hoping that dealing with Mathilde was going to be the easiest task for me to accomplish. Somehow, I didn't think it would be.

SALEX TAX

One thing that I was taught from a very young age, from various female family members, was that when apologising, it was best to arrive with gifts in tow. I figured that since I was apologising by proxy, that showing up with a bouquet of roses and a box of chocolates was in my best interest.

Mathilde lived in one of those nice apartment buildings with doorman who stared at you until you were allowed entrance, the big vaulted ceilings, the marble columns it looks like they were actual stone, and painted walls instead of atrocious wallpaper. In simple terms, her building was just as nice as Dermot's and had a little bit more in the way of classic luxury attached to it. It was the sort of place where you would expect to see people who were wealthy doing their best to show people that they were wealthy. In a word, it was trendy.

It must have been the flowers and chocolates that got me through the doorman's focused gaze. He had called her and described me as 'some guy with flowers is here for you'. Some muttering on the other end of the phone and I was let up. I went to the fourth floor, found apartment 407, pushed the buzzer, and was immediately taken aback.

The door opened before my hand could pull away from the buzzer and what I found was not at all salubrious to the friendly neighbourhood marketing agent who was just trying to lend his help to try and sort out a tax problem. It occurred to me as I hurriedly looked away from the woman wearing nothing but lacy lingerie and pointy shoes, that as much as I like to cling to the title of normal human, my life was anything but normal.

"You are not Ferdinand," Mathilde said. I kept my gaze to the ceiling, studying the pattern of paint there.

"No. I am not Ferdinand. My name is Cal Thorpe and your...husband? Husband. Your significant other... Dermot Green has sent me to apologise to you on bended knee for the unfortunate way he talked with you this morning over the phone." I held out the flowers and the chocolate, still doing my best not to look at her. There was silence for a moment. Out of the corner of my eye, I could see her moving, shifting her weight on those dangerous spikes stilettos, and probably considering some way to get rid of me.

"Since when does Dermot apologise?" Mathilde asked. She jabbed me in the chest, forcing me to look down and meet her gaze. I did my best to focus on her reddish, brownish hair, her generally pleasant features, the way her eyes glared daggers into me. I wasn't really interested in her—she was not only about fifteen years older than me, but I didn't much care for the calculating, predatory, seductive look that she was giving me. However, going to apologise for someone did not mean that I was prepared to face a woman wearing lingerie. I coughed.

"Perhaps we could talk inside? Or you could just put on some clothes…" I said, lifting my eyes once again to the ceiling.

"Sheesh. A woman opens the door wearing nothing but that and you have the gall to look away?" Al asked. I did not want to have that conversation right then. "You have some strange notions about politeness."

What I had were distinct urges to wrap my hands around Al's incorporeal throat and shake him. However, I did not want to appear insane in front of the person I had to charm enough to agree to go to dinner with her husband, so I said nothing and just waited.

"We can talk inside, provided you answer one question for me. Who are you and how did Dermot managed to contract you to do this?" Mathilde propped a fist on her hip and narrowed her eyes. She did not take the flowers or the chocolate, nor did she seem at all concerned by her lack of appropriate dress.

"My name is Cal Thorpe and I work for Death. Dermot…contracted me…through an obligation that I owed to parties unnamed," I said, trying to be as truthful as possible and yet as vague as possible. The question was all about how much power he was exerting in order to win her approval. It was classic posturing, at least for the denizens of Elsewhere, and if she found out that I was the one coercing him into participating in this course of action, then we would be in serious trouble. As it was, she seemed to believe me.

Of course, that brought on a whole different set of problems.

Her gaze narrowed in seduction, she licked her lips and shifted her posture ever so slightly. Suddenly, my embarrassment at having caught her en deshabille as it were vanished into annoyance. I really did not have time for this.

"You work for Death, do you? Did you know that a banshee is a caller for Death? That we wail and weep as a foretelling of Death's coming?" She took a step forward into the hallway, pressing her hand flat against my chest. I coughed again, looking around and half expecting someone to jump out and try to kill me or start yelling or something equally terrible.

"Yes, yes, that's all very nice. Look, can we go inside and discuss this with you fully clothed?" I didn't wait for an answer, I just pushed past her into the apartment and focused my attention on the furniture in the decor rather than Mathilde. I heard a huff and a sigh behind me, but the door clicked closed and the sound of heels on the wooden floor told me that she was complying. I had enough time to study a reproduction Monet print on the wall while she dressed.

"Very well, Cal. I am dressed. Now let us discuss what exactly it is that my husband wants from me this time." Mathilde sauntered past me in clothes that looked as though they had been painted on. She wore some sort of leather type leggings and a white T-shirt that clearly show the lingerie beneath. It wasn't much better, but there wasn't a whole lot I could do about it either.

I handed her the roses and the chocolates, which she took and rolled her eyes at before sauntering into the kitchen area. Mathilde gestured to the table and I sat. She sat across from me, crossing her legs and bouncing her foot so that the heel moved. If it was meant to be seductive, it failed. I could never figure out how women walked in those things. It looked more likely to break their ankles than allow them to move gracefully.

"As I said before, I am here on behalf of your husband in order to apologise for his unfortunate communication skills earlier today. He wishes to convey that he was sorry, that he just wanted to ask you out to dinner, and that he wishes to start making amends." I spread my hands in what I hoped was a gesture of openness and peace, and received nothing but a snort and return. Actually, I received two starts, one from Al who was hovering behind Mathilde.

"And do you have any idea why my husband actually needs to apologise? Did he conveniently leave that out of your contractual obligation to him?" Mathilde leaned forward, angling a bony shoulder in my direction, her features suddenly sharp and a bit terrifying.

"I was simply sent to convey a message, to allow him the chance to try and win you back." Please, please let that work. It was already mid-afternoon and I had a considerable amount to do to prepare for this evening.

Not to mention, the way Mathilde's stare turned angry was extremely disconcerting. I mean, realistically I knew that she wouldn't actually be able to do me any permanent harm—well any fatal damage—but I liked to work in a way that people liked me, they trusted me. I portrayed the best image of them and they believed that I would help them appear to be sometimes better than they were. I was a marketing agent. Public relations specialist. I dealt with perception, putting on a smile when things were bad, knowing precisely when to apologise and frown and to say something more serious. But that was about perception. And it was about other people. Rarely did I have to feel that sort of disconcerting anger directed actively at me. Even during my time in Elsewhere, people thought I was either strange because I was human, strange because I could not die, or they wanted something from me. They were rarely angry in my direction.

Just what had Dermot done?

"Let me explain to you something about Dermot Green," Mathilde said with a twist to her hand that looked straight out of some movie. "Dermot Green is a criminal. Not only that, he is a criminal who likes to be in charge. He likes to control the flow of information, the movement of product, the actions of others. It's what makes him such a good mobster. Because, let's face it, there really is no polite way to describe what it is that he does. And having all that power was part of what drew me to him. But when he starts to try to control *me,* when he thinks that he can say something and I will fall at his feet in gratitude for buying me dinner, or taking me out dancing, then we have a problem. See, I like to live *my* life precisely how *I* want. That means I can talk to whomever I wish, I can dance with whomever I wish, and I don't have to answer to him. Okay, yes, he is my husband, so I have to at least make my affairs discrete, but it's not just me that is the problem. He thinks he can control me while doing the exact same thing that other people. He is a womaniser, his eyes follow every woman that walks within twenty feet of him, no matter if they're ugly or human. No offence."

"None taken," I said. Being called human was the least of my worries right now.

"And then he does this thing where he obsesses over every little dime spent. I mean, like I don't know how to budget. I know full well what it takes to pay the mortgage on this place. To pay the utilities, deal with the car insurance. To pay off the mortal authorities. When I want to spend a little money on myself, when I want to go out and have a good time, to wear nice clothes and do nice things, what does he do? He starts complaining like I'm draining his bank account. I mean, there are images to maintain. Surely someone like you, someone who works for Death, knows full well the power that image holds. So I have to have my image, or I'll get no respect from humans or people from Elsewhere. And there Dermot is, trying to control every single penny that is spent. He thinks that going to one of those stupid chain restaurants, the Italian place or whatever is a good time. He thinks that that is a pricey meal. Have you seen his apartment? He can afford better than that. And yet he thinks that's all I'm worth. So I don't care if he wants to reconcile. I am tired of him controlling my life. Dermot Green? I say let them suffer."

Another one of those useful things that I have learned from various female relatives when I was growing up was that sometimes it was best to just let them talk, to get whatever it was off their chest. And then you apologise, even if it wasn't your fault. "I'm so sorry that you feel this way. It was of course never his intention to make you feel belittled or controlled. He merely has…Over protective tendencies. He is inclined towards jealousy when something that he loves is perhaps threatened…" I really wished I had watched more of that television show that Agravane was going on about. Maybe then I would actually understand what it was that I was supposed to say to make the situation diffuse.

"Jealousy?" Mathilde raised her brows and looked at me, pursing her lips into a confused line.

"Wild jealousy. He cannot stand the thought of you with someone else," I said. Al, ever helpful, leaned in next to my ear and I could practically feel his grin.

"Well done, Cal. It seems as though you have some hidden talents after all. I mean, besides your day job that you call poking at those computers. A few more sweet words and you'll have this dame eating out of your hand." Al clapped me on the shoulder, and I had a brief moment of wondering just how exactly he managed to do that considering that he didn't have a physical form. I mean, I could see him, but—really, Cal, concentrate on the situation at hand.

"If that's the case, then why does he have such a wandering gaze?" Mathilde lifted her chin, her expression all but proclaiming her victory.

I swallowed and did my best to give her a charming smile while I racked my brain for a plausible answer. "Um, well, that's simply because he wishes to make an objective assessment of whether or not any other woman could possibly measure up to you.…Of course they never do."

Al squeezed my shoulder tighter, and grinning like a manic idiot. I really needed to get him contained into some sort of mental cage. He was messing me up quite desperately.

Mathilde considered for a moment, studying me while I studiously did my best to ignore the mobster hovering at my shoulder. Then, she tossed her hair over her shoulder tilted her head back and laughed. And I knew then exactly why it was that people feared a banshee's cry. I thought it had been an exaggeration, that their wailing was going to be more like a sobbing teenager than a true, terror inducing event. But Mathilde's laugh was like nails grading on a chalkboard in the midst of a tree chipper, while tone deaf choirs were singing Bach. I wanted to clap my hand over my ears and managed to refrain.

Part of me, the part I figured was most influenced by Al Capone at that moment, understood perfectly why Dermot perhaps had a few problems in his relationships.

Mathilde clapped her hands over her mouth and I was a little surprised to see a blush covering her skin. "I so sorry. My wailing doesn't normally happen like that. It's to do with impending Death. But, surely you—"

"Please don't worry about it, it actually makes perfect sense. I work for Death after all." I didn't need to answer more questions about the fact that I couldn't I was currently under a Death curse from a djinn who had been accidentally directed to fire her magic at me. By Mathilde.

"You are an unusual man, Cal. You seem to actually be clever. Which, if I recall correctly, is the first time that Dermot has actually done something smart, in hiring you. Of course, I can't take his apology at face value unless he delivers it himself and shows me that he intends to act otherwise." Mathilde gave me another one of those superior glances, the arch look that people managed to give when they were offended or uncertain of being in the right. I didn't know if she was or she wasn't, but we were getting somewhere close to an agreement to go to dinner. Maybe.

"Naturally not," I said, reaching out and grabbing her hands, trying to play the sympathetic friend. It hadn't worked so well during my university days, but I was hopeful that I had evolved since then. "That is why he would like to invite you to dinner this evening. At La Casa de las Velas."

Mathilde sucked in a breath. "You can't get a reservation there unless you're ambitious and wealthy and famous. Not even a year in advance. Are you telling me that he—"

"He has," I said through clenched smiling teeth. "He'll meet you there at eight."

Mathilde squealed like an overeager teenager at a concert and clapped her hands excitedly. Thankfully, she didn't do her banshee wail again, instead sounding simply like an annoying woman. "Oh thank you! I am going to show Dermot precisely what he has been missing out on."

I nodded and continued to wear my smile, though my cheeks were starting to hurt. "In that case, then I show take my leave. I shall be assisting Dermot this evening, so I'll be sure to keep him in check."

I don't think Mathilde heard me. She was glancing at her shoes and studying them from a couple of different angles, an eager look in her eyes. I stood up from the table and walked backwards towards the door. I waved my goodbyes, trying not to draw her attention, and slipped out. Only when the door was closed firmly behind me and I was out of view of its people did I allow my shoulders to relax and the breath of relief at leaving leave me.

"Well done, Cal. You seem to have the touch with dealing with people. Too bad we didn't know each other when I was alive. I could have used a guy like you on my side." Al said, sauntering along with his hand stuffed into his pockets as though he didn't have a care in the world. I jabbed at the elevator button. "Even now, perhaps you can still be of particular use to me. I mean, I know I'm dead and all, but sending you my soul has given me a new perspective on living. And it reminds me just how much I missed it."

I whirled on Al, jabbing my finger into his face. He didn't even flinch. "I am using your soul temporarily so that I do not become a sociopathic zombie. I suggest that you keep in mind the fact that I have battled Life and Death and came out still standing. You are only a temporary nuisance. You are dead. And if you try to exert more influence on me, then I shall find a witch and bind you, and trust me you won't like the result."

I turned away from him and noticed that the elevator doors were open to the lobby and that a couple of people were glancing nervously in my direction. I straightened my shoulders and ignored them, walking out as though I had the confidence to say I owned the building. Al followed me, and I could feel his smug expression in the way his soul interacted with my emotions. I didn't know a witch. I didn't know whether a binding would work on him. All I knew was that I didn't need one more problem just then.

Of course, as soon as I thought the words, problems came my way. I had barely gotten out to the street and was just pulling out my phone to find a ride share when someone thrust a black bag over my head and shoved me into a van. There was a squeal of tires and the van lurched away from the curb, throwing my off-balance body weight to the side with a crash and a collection of new bruises for me to enjoy. The only thought I had before someone conked me on the head was that at least they hadn't tried to shoot me. Yet.

TAX REFORM

Now, I don't know about normal people, but as far as kidnapping events went for *me*, being grabbed and stuffed into the back of a van was perfectly ordinary. I had, so far, been transported by smoke with a vampire, taken into a cavern dungeon by an order of assassins, pulled through time…you get the picture. So when these people pulled me from the van and shoved me into a dingy metal chair—to which they tied my hands—I was feeling downright cheerful about the whole situation.

Then, they pulled off my hood.

I was in a warehouse. This was on the more grimy end of the warehouse scale, though there was nothing terribly interesting inside. Just cracked concrete floors and a few wilted cardboard boxes that had probably at one time contained something interesting. Or not. All of the windows were smashed in, leaving the broken glass scattered on the floor, and the steel girders that ran the length of the ceiling were well rusted. I was sitting on a really uncomfortable chair and the ties on my hands were too tight. None of that was terribly important, but it was useful to know as I faced down my kidnappers.

These people, I assumed, belonged to Dermot Green. Or, rather, they would until his deal with the feds came through and then they would belong to his lieutenant. Of the three people in the room—four if you considered Al who was wandering around admiring their guns—I figured the one with the slightly panicked expression wearing the red beanie and pointing a gun in my direction was probably him.

"What have you done to our boss?" the man demanded, waving his weapon at me. Well yes, he was definitely the lieutenant.

"How about some introductions first? Hi, my name is Cal," I said, and feeling perhaps more snarky than was wise in the current situation. Not that wisdom had ever stopped me from being snarky before.

To my surprise, it worked. "Cal, is it? You have no idea who you're messing with. I am Ricky Poole, second in command to Dermot Green. You know who he is, don't you? If the families here knew anything about the world of Elsewhere, they would be cowering at his feet. As it is, he has enough power to shut them down even with the mortal authorities."

Ricky leaned in, baring his teeth in an arrogant smile of some sort. Considering the way he was waving his weapon, almost carelessly, at me I figured that the bullet was probably going to be the next way I would meet my death. Somehow, the thought was a little reassuring. A bullet was perfectly ordinary. And probably less painful than being crushed by a piano.

"Good for him. Good for you. Is there a particular reason why you kidnapped me today? Or are you this aggressive with all strangers to the city of Chicago?" I asked, feeling snarky even for me. I snapped my eyes to Al, who shrugged.

"Trust me, kid, this one's all you. Though I do approve," Al said, standing next to one of the thugs. He reached out and waved his hand through the massive gun that this thug was holding, whistling low. "Technology sure has improved. And yet people still feel the need to shoot each other. I don't know whether to be pleased or disappointed."

Sometimes, it was a good thing that no one could see or hear Al. My inevitable death would come much sooner if they could hear him.

Ricky put his hands to his head, the gun pointing off into the distance. He looked as though he had taken my words at face value, rather than interpreting the sarcasm. I wondered if Dermot's assessment of his lieutenant was accurate. He seemed exactly the sort to call his boss at the first sign of trouble, but I wouldn't have necessarily called him capable. At least, he certainly didn't have any experience in the whole hostage questioning situation.

"Don't play games with me," Ricky said, jabbing the gun in my direction. Again. "I saw you with Green. I saw you with that cow he married. You know why he won't answer my calls. Why he won't deal with any of the product that we've been bringing in, were the family problems we've been having."

Product? I frowned. I knew that Dermot was a mobster and therefore ostensibly had his fingers in many distasteful pies, but something about having magical beings dealing drugs to normal humans rubbed me the wrong way. Possibly because they had so much power over people, even if the people didn't know they were. I decided right then that my goal would not just be to get Dermot to pay his taxes, but also to take this ridiculous group down.

"Oh, yes, I know exactly why it is that he won't return your calls. I know exactly why it is that he won't contact you about your product or about any of your family troubles," I said, drawing on some of Al's smugness to straighten my shoulders, lift my chin. "I'm surprised that you haven't figured it out yet. After all, you are second in command. Shouldn't you know exactly what it is that your boss is doing? Shouldn't you be…*capable* enough to step into his place?"

Ricky shifted his weight and looked between the two other thugs. One of them, the taller of the two with almost no hair and really ill-fitting clothes, shrugged. The skinnier thug, curled inward on himself, sniffed and shook his head. Al laughed, walking just behind him. "There you go, Cal. Don't let them see any weakness. Bluff your hand. Maybe you are a better poker player than I thought."

I gritted my teeth, trying my best to ignore Al. After all, I had beat him in poker. Now he was just trying to goad me into a reaction.

"What are you saying?" Ricky demanded. His brain had finally caught up with the situation. He stared at me wide-eyed, trying his best to splitter in anger though it wasn't really working for him. He just looked like a slightly annoyed terrier rather than the terror that he wanted to be. "I am the most trusted member of Dermot's team. I am like a brother to him. If he isn't telling you what's going on, it's because you got to him. Who do you work for? The feds? Another one of the families? Or are you here on some stupid errand from Elsewhere, trying to think that one of those idiots could muscle in on what we've got here."

I rolled my shoulders and heaved a dramatic sigh. "First off, if you're talking to the feds, they're not going to have any idea what the Elsewhere is. You're just going to come off as insane. Which, now that I think that might be useful if you're trying to portray a certain amount of criminal insanity for a defence of some sort. But, it does rather reveal a lot. And I'm fairly certain that most denizens of Elsewhere don't actually care to have their identity paraded about. It makes them vulnerable. And when vulnerable, they tend to lash out."

Ricky chuckled nervously, the gun once again pointed at me. "You can't lash out. You're tied to a chair. And if you had some sort of magical powers, surely he would have used them already. Instead, I think you're just trying to buy time. What, never been up against a red cap before?"

I tested my bonds again just to be sure. Yep. I was tied up. These idiots were my only way out of here. I had to get them to release me or I would be stuck here for a very long time, and my plans for this evening would be ruined.

"Actually, no. My experience with the Fae has been rather limited, though I understand that you are from the Celtic tradition. See, I have come into contact more with things like rock trolls and vampires and aurai. Not so much fairies." I gave my most charming smile, talking as though I were doing nothing more strenuous than putting together some background information for marketing profile. It infuriated Ricky.

"Yeah, well, you've been fortunate thus far. See, even among Faeries, I ain't so nice. Red caps kill people, see, and we soak our hats in their blood. To keep it red enough, we have to do this fairly frequently. I mean, dried blood just doesn't have the right colour."

As far as intimidation techniques went, this would have worked great if I had been a normal person. I wasn't a normal person. And I wasn't impressed. "Don't you just hate that? Colours fade, you have to keep things out of the sun, I mean my goodness. You know, you could just get a dye and make your hat whatever colour you want. It would be far more permanent than constantly soaking it in blood."

"Cal, you're starting to be stupid," Al said, walking towards me. He stopped just to the left of Ricky and examined the angry red cap with detached, almost psychopathic disinterest. He curled his lip in disdain. "While I normally approve of not showing fear, or giving into taunting, acting on those thoughts don't tend to end well for someone who is tied to a chair with no visible means of escape."

"Are you mocking me?" Ricky snarled, surging forward and grabbing my shirt in his fist, jabbing the gun against my chin with the other hand. I sneezed, something in his cologne really setting me off. This turned out to be one of the smartest things I could have done, because he recoiled, wiped desperately at his face amidst proclamations of disgust, then looked at the two thugs he had brought with him. They were holding back snickers, their eyes wide. Ricky roared and turned back to me, hitting me across the face with the pistol. My glasses flew off, but I didn't hear the cracking of the lens, so I figured they would be okay for a moment or two. I did taste blood in my mouth, and now mine whole left side of my face was throbbing. One downside of my particular "ability" was that I could sustain as many injuries as it would take for someone to get what they wanted from me, and I would only heal from the fatal ones. My jaw was going to be a bloom of bruises tomorrow.

I spit a globule of blood onto the ground then smirked at Ricky. "Oh yes, hitting a man tied to a chair, real dangerous."

Ricky roared again, beat me once more across the jaw, then decided that why mocking perhaps had some merit. He pointed his gun at me, then waved the tall thug over. "Untie him."

"Are you sure about this Ricky? We don't even know why it is that he's hanging out with Dermot. Maybe we should ask more questions—"

Ricky rounded on this thug, his gun still pointed in my direction. I couldn't see his expression, but if Al's raised brow was any indication, it was not good. "Are you questioning my orders?"

"Nah, Ricky. Just...thinking." The thug shuffled over to stand behind me and started fiddling with the knots at my wrist.

"Well don't." Ricky stood and pointed his gun at me. When the thug had finished untying me, he stepped back quickly, his own weapon trained me. Somewhere in the back of my mind, I wondered why it was that Neja's wish magic hadn't accidentally caused one of the guns to discharge at me. Was it opportunistic or just waiting for a particularly dramatic moment? I would have to ask her about how wish magic worked. Or rather, I would have to ask Agravane because I had a feeling Neja would just laugh at me and then walk away.

I stood from the chair, rubbing at my wrists. I walked over to where my glasses were on the floor, picked them up, blew off some dust, and replaced them on my face. Everything was suddenly so much clearer. I turned to look at Ricky, who was doing his best to look predatory. Once again, it didn't work.

"Okay, wise guy," Ricky said, taking a step forwards and pointing his gun at me execution style. "Let's see how tough you are now."

I dusted off my shirt and pants, taking my time. "Tough? Me? Oh not at all. You could beat me in a fight hands down. No, the whole point of this conversation was to get out of the chair so I could get back to going about my work, which at this particular time involves your boss. He doesn't know I'm here, does he?"

"I'll give you smarts for getting out of that chair, but now you're being stupid again," Al whispered in my ear. "We don't have time for heroics. And you're not strong enough to pull it off, either."

I elbowed Al in the gut, trying to make it look as natural as possible. I wasn't sure if my hit connected, considering that he was intangible, but I felt satisfaction of the action either way. When all of this was over and I was back at that ridiculously fancy hotel, I was going to take some time and have a very long conversation with Al about boundaries. And I was going to put him in a mental cage that was too small to move around in, and it would be wonderful if only for the fact that he would just shut up.

"Well no of course he doesn't know that you're here. We can't get him to answer our phone," tall thug said. I was beginning to like this guy.

"Shut. Up!" Ricky hissed at his subordinate. He took another step closer, waving his gun in my face. "You're telling me that you couldn't fight me? That you just wanted me to untying you? What do you take me for some sort of idiot?"

I said nothing, just raised my eyebrows as high as they would go and nodded. This had, generally, the desired effect. Ricky let out another one of those roars that was meant to scare you witless, then started shooting.

Weirdly, two bullets grazed my left shoulder, making it hurt substantially, but not killing me.

Another embedded itself in my right hip, which did elicit a scream of pain, but again did not kill me. The other bullets ricocheted around the room, embedding themselves in the walls and, importantly, the steel girders that ran the length of the ceiling.

By the time the shooting was done, I was on the ground with my left arm screaming in pain and my right hand pressed against my hip as I tried to take deep breaths and work through the discomfort. I had been in worse situations than this, but the pain usually didn't last quite this long. I didn't like it. Ricky was standing over me, clicking the trigger on an empty barrel, his face turning quite red and splotchy. He looked as though he was going to yell out something to one of his thugs, probably demanding their guns or more bullets or something so that they could kill me, but he was stopped by something more pressing.

One of the girders started creaking ominously.

As one, all of us turned to look up at the ceiling. One of the girders, incidentally the one directly above me, seem to have been held to the ceiling by a particularly rusted bolt. I was surprised it hadn't come down before then. But, in the fighting, Ricky's bullets had—magically—managed to hit that one last point of connection. It was going to fall, and it was going to fall on me.

Perhaps my next death would not be quite so ordinary after all.

"Run!" This was from the tall thug, the thinker of the group. The other two followed his orders without question, turning and scrambling out of the way as quickly as they could. I, being shot, was not so quick. Even though I knew it would happen, the sensation of being crushed under a steel girder while already being shot in the hip and arm was something that I didn't particularly like. The piano had killed me almost instantly, crushing my skull first. The girder landed on my spine and caused my ribs to shatter inwards, puncturing my lung. I lay gasping on the ground, many bones in my body broken, bleeding out, and waiting for that inevitable moment when I crossed the barrier of death. It didn't take as long as I thought, given how dramatic some of these things seems to be in television shows. A matter of moments and I was faced with the usual flash of white light, and then I woke up again completely whole. And still pinned by the steel girder.

"You do seem to find yourself in unusual situations." I lifted my head as far as I could manage and saw Neja sauntering towards me, looking superior and somewhat like an angel sent to help me. Though I imagine she often took the role of avenging angel rather than helpful neighbourhood guide.

"This one is new. Would you mind helping me get out of here?" I asked, pushing at the ground as hard as I could and unable to turn to get any leverage on the girder. Neja smiled and crouched down in front of me. She reached out and brushed some of my hair back from my forehead. It felt like sparks jumped from her skin to mine, and I did my best not to wince.

"I charge an extra two hundred for chivalrous acts of assistance. Shall I put it on the itemised receipt?" She was teasing me. I think.

"For getting me out from underneath the steel girder, I will happily pay you two hundred dollars, and I will take you to dinner for steak." The last bit was meant more as a joke than anything, a desperate plea for her to actually hurry up. Neja instead took it at face value and grinned widely, her eyes flashing a bit more inhumanly than otherwise.

"You have yourself a deal, Cal Thorpe." She snapped her fingers and the girder was lifted from me, then shoved a few feet away. I collapsed to the ground, groaning. Those things weighed a tonne and they were not very comfortable, even if the fatal injuries had been healed, taking the gunshot wounds along with them. My muscles felt like they had been compressed and then stretched out on a rack, and my bones were complaining loudly in several different keys.

I stood and dusted myself off, wincing at each movement. Neja rose and watched me, her arms folded. I couldn't quite tell what her expression meant, and that terrified me just a little. She was obviously very powerful, and she had made my offer of a steak dinner sound like something she actually wanted. I really had no idea what women were thinking most of the time, and she seemed more mysterious than most. It was disconcerting.

"So why is it that all of the gun waving and bullets flying the went on, and I was killed by a steel girder crushing me?" I asked, limping towards the entrance. Neja shrugged and threaded her arm through mine, the action more possessive than it was endearing.

"That's easy. When using the wish magic, our Mrs.

Green pointed at you and said 'crush him dead'. So that is what the wish magic is doing. It's rather specific that way." Neja patted my arm like she was comforting a child. I huffed.

"Right. Because being the target of magic that wants me dead couldn't be easy, could it?"

Neja turned to grin on me, this one predatory end with more pointed teeth than seemed perhaps healthy. "Now you're getting into the spirit of things!"

TAX EVASION

By the time I got back to the ridiculously expensive hotel that I was desperately fond of, I was exhausted, had ruined another set of clothes, and things seemed to be going well in the planning for date night. At least, Agravane hadn't called me and told me that Dermot had run away screaming, so I thought things were doing alright. Neja had delivered me some information after releasing me from the warehouse and was now off doing who knows what. I didn't ask and I wasn't sure I wanted to know.

Who was I kidding? I wanted to know. I wanted to figure out what exactly a supernatural bounty hunter and private investigator did, not to mention that Neja was someone beyond my understanding and I, for better or worse, was curious. Curiosity had gotten me into my current job and unfortunate situation, so I wasn't certain it was a terribly healthy habit. But it was hard to kick.

I still had a few things to deal with to prepare for

date night, but I couldn't very well walk around the streets of Chicago dressed like a murder victim. Even the hotel staff looked at me a bit askance as I shuffled my way to the elevator, wearing an oversized T-shirt that I had picked up on some tourist kiosk to cover the blood stains on my shirt. Thank goodness the trousers were dark enough to hide any overt signs of trauma.

We went up to the room and took a shower, dressing and collapsing on the really, really nice bed. My eyes started to flutter close, but I couldn't give into the allure of plush mattresses and down pillows.

"You've been quiet for a while," I said, keeping my eyes closed.

"What do you want me to say? You seem to have everything well under control for a guy who is completely unconcerned with the safety of his skin. You don't need my help putting together this ridiculous charade of romance." Al sounded more or less upset, his words a little sharper than his normally lazy accent would suggest.

"I'm not dragging you around with me because I want your assistance," I said, sitting up and leaning back against the pillows. Al was standing, hovering, whatever at the foot of the bed, his hands in his pockets and his shoulders deceptively relaxed.

"Oh, yes, that's right, you're dragging me around because you find it useful to beat me at poker and gain use of my soul." Al pulled out a hand and snapped his fingers and I got the distinct impression that he was annoyed at me.

"Exactly. I need you because my soul is missing, and

if I do not have possession of a soul, then I turn into an emotionless being whose free will becomes lost in a cloud of disinterest. I have little desire to be an emotionless zombie, a being that requires constant ordering in order to fulfil normal tasks. Not to mention that I would be just as inclined to kill you as I would to keep you alive. That is one of the problems with losing your soul. You lose yourself." I pulled off my glasses and cleaned them as best I could. I wouldn't be able to get another pair for several days, so I had done my best to at least clean them properly, even if one of the lenses was cracked.

"Why are we having this conversation?" Al asked, looking at me with disdain. He circled the bed, attempting to brush his hand along the surface of the covers, though it passed right through his flesh. Annoyance crossed his features for a brief moment and then was gone. I leaned forward, studying him.

"You thought that giving me temporary use of your soul would be like being alive again. You want to be living. You wanted to be in the real world." That explained a lot, actually. It explained his covert influence on me, his comments to me about how best to deal with the situation. Al wanted to return to the world, and he thought I was his conduit.

"You think you know Life and Death simply because you can't die," Al snarled. He crossed through the bed so that he was standing in the middle of the mattress, his eyes flashing fire, his scar seeming more visible than before. "I was cheated out of my life. Sentenced to prison for something so stupid as tax evasion. I do know that I died there, from a disease that I picked up from some woman in a moment of lunacy. I didn't get to grow old with my wife, I didn't get to see my empire reached the heights that it could have done. I didn't get put my name on the world the way that I wanted. You know what they remember me for now? I'm the idiot who was arrested for tax evasion."

I think if Al had been able to interact with the world on a physical level, he probably would have killed me. Somehow, this thought disturbed me more than the two assassination attempts that day had done. I sucked in a breath and held it for a few moments, attempting some sort of meditative breathing like I had learned from Yolanda and the very few yoga sessions I had done as a living being, what seemed like a lifetime ago. When I released the breath, Al was still standing in the middle of the bed, his body truncated by the mattress, like a ghost.

"How about you don't stand there, first of all," I said. "Let's go sit at the table, before you give me even more of a headache."

Grumbling, the dead gangster complied. We sat at the table where Agravane and I had planned our course of action just that morning. Had really been just that morning? Al put his hands on the table, clenching them into fists and resting his weight on his elbows. I leaned back in my chair and studied him for a moment more.

"No matter how much you want it, Al, you are never going to get another chance at life. Even possession won't let you be alive again, just in temporary possession of touch."

He glared at me, lowering his brows until I was fairly certain he was going to lean forward and try to strangle me. He didn't, instead just tightening his fists further. "And what do you know about such things, Mr. Human? Your experience with magic is limited, your knowledge of the arcane legends has so many holes that you could see daylight. I've been dead a lot longer than you've been alive, or whatever you are. Don't tell me what is and isn't so."

"Fine. I'll concede your point. But do you honestly think that even if you manage to get a life, a new one, that it will be any more fair in your last one? Have you never met Life?" And my words, Al finally lowered his gaze. I pressed my advantage for as long as I held it. "Life is not fair. She's beautiful and tempting and thrilling and wonderful and we cling to her with everything we've got, but she is not fair. Never fair. She can be cruel, vicious, spiteful, but she will never, ever be fair."

"You only say that because you work for Death. You work for the terror that haunts people's nightmares. And you don't seem to be bothered by that in the slightest," Al shot back. Now here was something I did know a little about. After all, a good marketer couldn't put together a proper campaign without knowing this client, and I knew mine.

"Death is not the *enemy*. People are afraid of him because they do not know him. They do not know what comes afterwards. But that even is not his purview. He simply releases us. Perhaps kindly, perhaps not. You don't trust people, Al. Fine. But if you don't stop trying to manipulate your way into my activities, that we're going to have a problem. Because if my will is pitted against yours, I'm going to come out the winner." With that, I leaned forward myself, forcing Al to meet my gaze or look away.

I will give him credit, he tried. But if there was one thing that I had learned in my time working for Death and all of the strange things that came along with that, was that I was incredibly stubborn. I had put myself against beings who were hundreds of years older than me. I had stood opposed to the Order of Silence, an organisation dedicated to the balance between Life and Death and themselves assassins. I had fought Justice. I had stood between Life and Death when they were trying their best to obliterate each other. Okay, yes, most of this was born out of perhaps hopeful stupidity that I could make a difference when the forces of the universe were in play, when politics and machinations that had been around for centuries longer than me were moving. But my hopeful stupidity was backed up by a lot of stubbornness, and I wasn't going to let some gangster stare me down.

After about thirty seconds, Al looked away. He slammed a fist onto the table, his hand falling halfway through. With a hiss of disgust he pulled back. "I don't know what to make of you, Cal. You seem to just let the world throw you where it may, never actually planning things out. You don't seem to care whether or not someone uses that miraculous gift of yours to never die. You don't even try to fight. You just seem to know you're going to win."

I shrugged. "I've never been any good at fighting. Not really. But I am very good at talking to people. Maybe I'm smarter than some, maybe not. And, okay, I do use my inability to die to my great advantage. But I wouldn't be able to do half of the things that were required of me if I didn't believe that I was going to come out on top."

We fell silent for a few moments, neither of us quite sure what to say to the other. I still had to deal with Al, still had to make him see that he couldn't just try and exert his influence on me, couldn't try to make me more like him, more determined to be in charge, take control, to see the people ducking their heads in obeisance as I rose to the top. Nor did I think that he would willingly give up, even after this discussion. Al obviously wanted to be alive again a whole lot more than I had expected.

"Who are you, Cal Thorpe, to be so sure of your place in the world?" Al finally demanded. Again, I shrugged.

"I'm just me. Marketing agent, public relations specialist, someone who knows that perception matters to people. I may be a bit nonstandard, but not everyone can be the sword-toting hero."

Al Capone narrowed his eyes at me and I had a feeling that he hated me just then. There wasn't anything I could do about that.

Before I could continue my conversation without all and try to exact from him a promise to not cause quite so much trouble, the door to the hotel room burst open. Or rather, it swung open quite gracefully, letting

Agravane in followed by Dermot Green. Dermot looked a little nauseous. Agravane looked more annoyed than anything else.

"Mr. Green's federal contacts want to have a meeting. Tonight. At 8 o'clock." Agravane informed me.

It took me a moment to process that, but when I did, I jumped out of the chair and practically shouted at Dermot. "Seriously?! Right when your date is supposed to happen. If you don't show up, your wife is going to be severely upset. And you can bet that you will be spending the next century, perhaps more, at the beck and call of the Taxman."

Dermot held up his hands, eyes wide and mouth hanging slightly open. "This is not my fault. The feds are finalising my deal on Saturday, but there are a great deal of things to work out. Not to mention, there little nervous considering there was an uptick in chatter and activity in the warehouse district."

Well, that was not my fault either, but I could take some of the blame. I had never dealt with the federal government, but if television was at all accurate—and Agravane certainly seems to think so—then I was not surprised that they were nervous. I pinched my nose. Took a breath.

"Call them. Tell them that you can't come to the meeting, that you have a few final details to sort out before you go into the program, or you will be in serious trouble otherwise, with everything they planned compromised before they can get their hands on you. Tell them something, anything that will get you out of having to meet with them. Meet tomorrow.

Meet after the date. Just not during." I realise that I had stepped towards Dermot until he was a metre away, looking as though I were perhaps one of the more frightening things he had seen all day.

"Before the feds called," Dermot said, swallowing nervously, "Ricky Poole, my lieutenant, sent me a message. He's been trying to reach me."

"Oh yes, I am aware of your lieutenant and his efforts to reach you." Why wasn't he pulling out his phone and dialling the federal people?

"Ricky said that you fought them off, that you had him doing things he would never have otherwise done just with a few words and a threatening look. And he also said that you survived a firefight." He shuffled his feet, watching me with some sort of strange fear and admiration in his eyes. For a mobster, he really wasn't that terrifying. Or perhaps he just acknowledged that this was not the time and place for posturing. Or perhaps…perhaps he was truly afraid of me.

"You saw me get flattened by a piano and survive, and you're more concerned about the fact that your lieutenant tried to shoot me and I didn't die? I think you need to focus on getting ready for your date. And that starts with you calling you whoever it is that you're communicating with, and getting them to meet you tomorrow." At this point, I had pulled out my own phone and was just about to hand it to him, just to get him to do what I asked. I didn't need one more thing trying to mess up this date night.

Dermot finally seemed to take me seriously and pulled out his phone from his pocket, dialling a number and wandering off to a corner of the hotel room. Agravane looked as though he was interested in starting a conversation, but I held up my hand and listened in on Dermot's half of his exchange.

"Yeah, it's me. Look, I know you want to meet up tonight, but...Yes I understand that Saturday is the last...Oh, well, there's nothing I can do about that. After Saturday, Friday night even, I won't have any more communication with...No there's nothing I'm holding back. As soon as the papers are signed and I am officially in your custody, then I won't cause any more problems. You will have every piece of information to deal with my people, and as much information as I have on the other families. I promise. But, that means that I have a few more days to tie up loose ends. And that means that tonight I can't meet with you...Well, no, I'm not meeting with my people." Dermot tugged his collar, looked over his shoulder at where Agravane and I were watching, and then turned back to study the picture on the wall.

"Yes, it's essential. I'm...I'm meeting my wife. Yes, of course, I'm married. If you had done any ounce of research, then you would have—oh, yes, we are estranged. But...I can't just disappear without informing her of something, or things are going to... Well haven't you ever had an angry woman try to hunt you down and kill you? Don't answer that. Look, all I'm asking is to meet up tomorrow morning instead of tonight. Okay? What you mean you want to talk to the guy who's been following me around all day...Have you been following me? I swore I would cooperate. There's no need to keep an eye on me. Look, fine, I will bring him to tomorrow's meeting. Okay?"

Dermot held the phone away from his year and grumbled in annoyance. He turned back to Agravane and myself, looking a little sheepish. At least he had that much sense. "Look, I can meet tomorrow instead of tonight, but only on the understanding that you go with me."

"Me?" I frowned, thoroughly confused. "Why in the world would they want to talk to me?"

"They've seen you around, hanging out with me and with Ricky and that djinn, and they don't know you. They think you're some sort of new player, trying to muscle in on my territory, making a deal with me to take control when I'm gone. They don't like it." Dermot rubbed the back of his head, messing up his hair and rather a dramatic fashion.

"Oh for goodness sakes. Fine. I will go with you. And I shall explain to them that I am just concerned about taxes."

To my surprise, Agravane was the one who snickered at that. "They won't believe that you're just here about taxes. You're staying in one of the most expensive hotels in the city, you're wearing custom made Italian suits, and one of your glasses lenses is broken. Trust me, you're not going to be interested in taxes. Not to them."

I was even more confused at that statement than the other. I looked down at my suit, which I thought was very nice and perfectly tailored, one of the few perks I allowed myself as Death's marketing agent. Not that the people of Elsewhere really appreciated well tailored clothing. At least, not of the human variety of clothing. "What's wrong with my suit?"

"Between that suit, your scowl, the broken glasses, and the fact that you haven't used one tax term since finding me in that café, you look far more like a mobster then you do a taxman, even to us folks from Elsewhere. And these feds aren't from Elsewhere. There purely human."

Agravane reached out and put his arms on my shoulders, a mockingly sympathetic look on his face. "Face it, boss man. You are becoming a force to be reckoned with. It means you won't be blending in quite as well from here on out, but the benefits will eventually outweigh the downsides."

In simple terms, Agravane was saying that I looked more dangerous than benign.

"And when is it eventually?"

Considering this day had started with me waking up in Elsewhere and then charging off to meet with the Taxman, ending up in a really nice restaurant after a day of trials and tribulations didn't seem like an awful thing. Of course, it would have been better if I had been able to actually enjoy my meal, instead of watching the table next to me for any sign that this date wasn't going as planned.

Agravane and I were sitting at one table, with Agravane taking notes as I said them, preparing for whatever the next stage of this plan would be. Personally, I was hoping that it would end sooner rather than later, whether that meant divorce or the exact opposite. Given that our deadline was Saturday, and we had already lost one day and were about to lose another dealing with the federal types, things were not moving fast enough. At a table directly across from the one where Dermot waited for Mathilde, Neja sat, wearing a black cocktail dress which showed off her legs, and not seeming at all bothered by the fact that her grey skin didn't at all blend in. My experience was that people would ignore unusual things until it was impossible to do so, but I also had a feeling that Neja was wearing a glamour or guise of some sort. Despite all their power and prowess, the supernatural magical community didn't much like gathering the attention of the more numerous and highly volatile humans.

Humans were many beings' prey, but they were the prey that fought back. And fought back well.

Dermot sat at the table between us, dressed in a dinner jacket and bowtie. He was perhaps a little over-dressed considering that this restaurant and catered to the trendy and dinner jackets were not trendy, but the supremely wealthy didn't tend to care about whether or not they were over or under dressed. Dermot looked a little uncomfortable, his hand reaching up every few seconds to tug at the bowtie—which at my insistence was a real bowtie instead of the clip-on one that Agravane tried to provide. It was three minutes past eight and Mathilde had yet to appear.

"Look, Cal, can we at least order food?" Agravane asked, looking at his menu one more time. I had glanced at it and found Spanish and Portuguese food of excellent quality, and no prices. This was not encouraging. Considering that I was paying for Dermot, Neja, and my own table's expenses, I sort of didn't want to know the price. Nor did I want to spend more than was really necessary. At this point, I was resigned to having to explain rather a lot to Death, and I hoped that he had a good sense of humour. Dermot couldn't get access to his funds, Neja was technically working for me, and well, Agravane and I did have to eat.

"Fine. Order food." I had barely given my acquiescence when Agravane waved over the waiter who had been patiently waiting for us to decide on our meal for the last fifteen minutes. Agravane spouted off a flurry of different food names, the waiter furiously writing them down. After what seemed like an interminable list, the waiter turned to me. I shrugged. Pointed to my menu at random and showed the waiter. His eyes widened ever so slightly and he straightened his shoulders, a look of pleased astonishment passing over his features.

"An excellent choice, sir," he said. He whisked away our menus and strode off. I returned my attention to Dermot's table.

"Here she is." Agravane got my attention and jerked his head towards the front of the restaurant. It was perfectly in character for Mathilde. That is, she made an entrance.

Unlike Neja's black cocktail dress, which was both attractive and tasteful, Mathilde had gone in the entirely opposite direction. She wore a red dress that clung to every twist and turn of her body, ending at mid thigh and hardly moving when she walked. It was designed to show off, well, everything, and instead managed to just draw confused attention. The neckline was too low, the back looked like it was restricting her breathing, and the fabric itself was made of some sort of strange shimmery material that looked like it belonged in a B science fiction movie.

Agravane snickered.

Dermot straightened, putting on a smile that was wide and slightly unbelievable, but perhaps the best he could do under the circumstances. As instructed by Agravane, he rose from the table and held out Mathilde's chair for her, taking her hand and kissing it rather than kissing her,. Mathilde looked a little baffled by this, as if she were unused to such attention.

"I told you. They expect to be stared at when they wear a dress like that, or are quite so spectacular divas as she seems to be, but they don't expect respect and admiration. That is the way to win the woman's heart, though your idea certainly helps." Agravane took a sip of his drink, some cocktail thing, with a smug look. I did my best not to give him a snarky response.

My idea was what Dermot next presented to Mathilde, sliding the velvet box over to her and main-taining eye contact while he did so. My theory was that for such beings as divas like Mathilde, that they expected a certain amount of, well, gild in their life. Judging by the book of astonishment when she opened the jewellery box and pulled out the ridiculously expensive and ostentatious necklace of red garnets surrounded by Swarovski crystal, I was not wrong. That did not mean Agravane was not wrong, just that it took all sorts.

"Where in the world did you get the money to afford this necklace, let alone a night out like this? Have you been holding things back from me Dermot?" Mathilde asked. I winced into my own drink, a very simple and dry red wine.

"I simply exerted some influence, calling in a few favours that I owed, the last ones that I have. You were absolutely worth every favour. And I would do it again until I was nothing more than a nameless fetch in service of the Lords of Faerie." Dermot reached for her hand. Mathilde beamed, the words apparently just right. Well, it seems that Dermot did know how to charm his wife. Whether or not he could do it long enough to get what we needed was a different matter altogether. But, with the next century of his life at stake, he was perhaps highly motivated.

The next hour was basically a study in over-the-top flirtation and wooing. Any time that Dermot started to get perhaps a little aggravated or frustrated with the comment made by Mathilde, referencing his difficult nature or jealousy, I coughed loudly, reminding him of his duty. Neja would occasionally do the same, for comments that I found relatively annoying but benign. Between the three of us keeping an eye on things, Dermot managed to get through the entire meal without too much incident.

There was one moment, when the waiter brought out my food that I almost caused incident myself. Apparently, when I had ordered the food, I had pointed to the largest and most expensive slab of meat that they offered. It was dressed with rice, peppers, beans, and was spiced to large measure. I poked at it with my fork and knife.

"How in the world is someone meant to eat all of this? Surely they can't be expecting that I would—"

"You should have let me order for you boss," Agravane said around a mouthful of what looked to be a very nice pasta dish. He pointed his fork at my meat. "You won't like that. Too much spice, not enough flavour."

Defiantly, I cut into my meal and took a bite. A moment later and I was coughing, causing Dermot some confusion and almost forcing Agravane over to beat my back. I swallowed the food and drink down as much water as I could, wheezing.

"When all this is over," I said through gasping breath, "I want a holiday. A proper holiday."

Agravane snickered and returned to his meal, keeping an eye out on Dermot stable while the man said something that had Mathilde laughing loudly.

"You don't want to hear from me," Al said, the first time that he had spoken up all evening, after our discussion earlier. He looked longingly at my meal. "I know you don't want to hear from me, but carelessness like that, like ordering food without knowing what it is, like coughing loudly in the middle of a situation where cough could mean many different things…carelessness and mistakes, they're going to cause you problems."

I glared at the gangster and defiantly cut another—smaller—piece of my meal, eating it by means of chewing very carefully. I swallowed and decided that the burning sensation inside my mouth was more in my head than a physical reality. Surely no food could be that ridiculous.

The sad part was that I was right. The careless mistake like the picking of food that made me cough when Dermot was relying on my coughs to signal him could have been potentially ruinous. If the situation were more dire than date night, then the consequences would be phenomenally bad. Maybe he was right. Maybe I was being too careless since I wasn't afraid of dying. What would happen when I got my soul back? I would probably be dead within a day if I didn't learn to be careful now.

This sufficiently darkened my mood until I was practically glowering at Dermot and Agravane. Even with all of that, things seem to be going well. Mathilde was smiling, laughing even, touching her neck and tilting her head to show off her new necklace, looking at Dermot instead of the other men in the restaurant. Things were going well. And I felt a little sad for it.

For all that they were a fetch and a banshee, Dermot and Mathilde had a relatively normal life. They were going to age normally, experience life in the mortal realms almost the same way that any other human did. Okay, most humans didn't get into organised crime, nor did they have the ability to foresee Death. But they were, relatively speaking, normal.

That used to be me.

About halfway through this date night, I pushed back from the table and muttered that I was going to the restroom to Agravane, stalking off to the back of the restaurant and trying not to glower at the waiter who had brought me that ridiculous meal. I found myself in a back hallway, a little separate from the rest of the restaurant, quiet and still. I leaned up against the wall, tilting my head back and closing my eyes.

"Things are going well."

I open my eyes and watched as Neja walked towards me, the dress or the shoes or something making it seem more like a saunter than a casual walk. She smiled and leaned next to the wall beside me.

"Indeed they are. Your discovery of her favourite gemstone was particularly useful. Thank you." My voice sounded stilted even to me. Neja snorted and shook her head, the white strands shining silver in this indoor lighting.

"Wow. Agravane was right. You are bad in normal conversation. How is it that someone who is so spectacularly good at marketing—oh yes I've looked you up Mr. Cal Thorpe—how is it that someone like you who can make everyone else look good can be so bad at it himself?" Neja turned to look at me, smirking just a touch. I tried not to grumble.

"Other people are easy. Then, it's a matter of me making them look good. Like with tonight with Dermot. Classic clothes, sparkly gift, making sure that his eyes never leave hers for more than a few moments, it all makes him look good. Which makes her look good. Which makes everything work out." I shrugged.

"You know how to make other people look good, but you don't how to make yourself look good? I mean, besides the tailored suits and the stylish glasses." Neja folded her arms and looked up at me, this time most definitely smirking. "You are very unusual. I like you. I see why Death likes you. Now if you could only figure out your feet in the world of Elsewhere, as it were, then perhaps we might get somewhere. I have never really spent all that much time with a human who knew what was what."

"Well I wouldn't say that I know everything. Or most things. But I'm glad that I can keep you entertained." I tried my best to smile at Neja, not entirely sure where this strange discomfort was coming from. Okay yes, some of it was coming from the fact that I found her incredibly beautiful and didn't quite know what to do with that. I mean more than your usual beautiful immortal beastie sort of beautiful. But part of it was, I think, due to the fact that I wasn't the same human who was originally hired by Death. Agravane's comments earlier about me perhaps becoming more powerful, more dangerous, they had set me on edge. In life, I had wanted only one thing: to be successful at my marketing job, to have a reputation for the best marketing work. I wanted to do something and I wanted to do it well. I didn't much care about power, except that it proved that I was capable. I certainly didn't care about being dangerous.

Now, somehow, I was on my way to both.

Neja looked like she was going to say something when an outraged shout from the restaurant interrupted us. She and I exchanged a look and dashed back out to where a relatively calm date night had turned into another episode of this month's soap opera.

Again.

Mathilde was glaring daggers at Dermot, her drink having recently been emptied onto his shirt, his face still dripping. Dermot was spluttering, looking a little like a drowned rat. His face shifted, taking on some of

Mathilde's features, and I knew things were about to get really bad.

"Don't you dare try to pull your doppelgänger magic on me." Mathilde snarled. "You forget that we are both harbouring or this, heralds of Death." Her voice was becoming a little shrill, little too inhuman. People in the restaurant were starting to look alarmed. I strode from the back hallway, lifting my shoulders as I did so, figuring that I might as well play on whatever potentially dangerous attributes I had going for me. As I approached the table, the waiter that had been sent to try and calm things between the two arguing restaurant goers looked a little relieved and backed away.

"Is something the matter here?" I asked in my best polite yet threatening manner. Actually, I tried to emulate Death. It seemed to work. Dermot quickly hid his face in his napkin, wiping off the remains of the margarita. Mathilde looked at me for half a moment and then looked away, having the grace to blush. Although, it could have just been anger.

"He had the gall to ask me about talking to her lawyers, seeing if we can put this nonsense about our finances behind us. As if one decent date could possibly make up for everything that has gone wrong in the last six months." Mathilde's hand tightened into fists and I saw her looking furtively towards her silverware.

"I see," I said darkly, turning my glare to Dermot. He gave a half shrug, as if a verbal apology was just too much work for him.

"I was just…I was just thinking that if things were better between us now, then maybe we didn't need to worry about all the lawyers, maybe we could sort out our problems between ourselves. I mean...Life is short and we don't always know how much time we've got. I would rather spend it with you then trying to...uh... argue with lawyers." Dermot stumbled over his words, casting his eyes around as he tried to come up with a decent excuse for what he had said. He had obviously said it because he wanted Agravane and myself gone, because he wanted to get out of the life without any more baggage holding him down, and this was the way he thought to do that. Well, it didn't work.

Mathilde, who had happily lapped up every sappy comment that Dermot had foisted her way during the pleasanter portion of the evening, narrowed her eyes. "Do you honestly think I am that stupid? There's something else going on here." She pointed at me. "You never owed a favour to my husband, did you? No, I think he owed a favour to you, and is going about it the best way that he can."

"He does not, nor ever has, owed me a favour." I lifted my chin, as if such a thought were completely preposterous. It was, but I don't think she believed me.

"So, what," Mathilde said narrowing her eyes further at Dermot, "this is some elaborate ploy to win me back because you want to spend the rest of your life with me, because you're desperately in love with me?"

For once, Dermot said something right. "I've always loved you, Mathilde. Maybe too much. Maybe that's why I can't stand you even looking at another man. Our personalities clash quite a lot, but that doesn't mean I haven't loved you."

"Well I haven't always loved you. You're a boor." Mathilde lifted her nose and gazed down as best she could her estranged husband. To be fair, I didn't think she was wrong. He had been so far self-serving and unafraid of the consequences of his actions. But he hadn't seemed like a bad guy, all things considered.

"I know, and I deserve that. But does that mean that I can't try to win you back? That all hope is lost for me?" Dermot reached out a hand, looking hopeful. It seemed to be an unusual look for him, one that his features were not used to making. That made it all the more sincere.

Mathilde took a breath, looking between Dermot, myself, and the table. She shook her head. "No, it doesn't mean that you can't try."

She reached out to take his hand, and I figured at this point that the two of them deserve some sort of fireworks or something to celebrate their rekindling of a relationship. What they got instead was Ricky and his two thugs, followed by a couple more people, walking into the restaurant with their weapons openly displayed, staring right at Dermot Green.

Behind me, Neja cursed. I was inclined to agree.

Weirdly, the restaurant staff were the first ones to react. Dermot was standing with his mouth hanging open, Mathilde was still seated, her mouth hanging open, Neja and I were standing still—our mouths were not hanging open but our expressions were similarly shocked—and Agravane was, well, still sitting and acting perfectly calm. One had to recall that he had been trained by a group of finely trained assassins, and that he was very fond of a good meal.

"Good evening, Sirs," a short woman said, wearing all black with a name badge. She was probably the manager. She peered up at Ricky, her expression inscrutable. "We ask that all customers refrain from open carry weapons within the confines of the restaurant."

Ricky adjusted to the cap on his head, looking between his various groupies and trying to figure out what to do next. He really wasn't all that good at thinking for himself. "Look here, lady," Ricky said, his hand flashing dangerously near his weapon. "We're not here to cause trouble. We just want to talk with a friend of ours."

"Be that as it may, sir, we ask that if you wish to continue openly carrying your weapon that you do so outside. We shall send your friend out to meet with you. May I have his name?" The woman's hand reached for a phone, probably ready to dial the cops. If someone else hadn't already done so. I doubted it was restaurant policy to give up their customers to people carrying weapons. Which meant that this was now a hostage situation.

The slightly more intelligent thug from earlier spoke, eyeing the customers in the restaurant warily. I was a little surprised that no one had broken out screaming or shouting, but then these were people who worked very hard to keep their cool under just about any circumstance. That, and no one had actually drawn a weapon. Yet. "We don't want any trouble. Were not can hurt them. We just want a chance to talk to Dermot Green."

This could have gone fairly well, given that it was a decently polite hostage negotiation—not that I have a great deal of experience with those things. Most of my hostage situations involved myself being taken hostage, summarily executed and then come back, usually with much screaming and wailing. On my side. For once, not being the target was almost nice. Until I remembered that if I lost Dermot my tenure with the Taxman would go on for rather a long time. As I said, this could have gone fairly well, with everyone being calm and reasonable, but I hadn't taken into account the fact that Mathilde was becoming more or less enraged.

"What is going on here, Dermot? You brought your work to our date night? I thought you would hit a new low with talking about money of all things. But no, instead, your gang shows up." Mathilde shoved her chair back, the wood squeaking along the floor in that horrid noise. She glared at Dermot, folding her arms and sticking one hip out.

"Look, Mathilde, it's really not what you think. Tonight was just supposed to be about us, supposed to be about you and me forever." Dermot held up his hands, looking a little more frightened of his wife than his wayward employees.

"Sir?" The restaurant manager said with one single eyebrow raised, her voice unimpressed. "Do you know these men? Do you want to go with them? If so, we ask that you please exit the restaurant as soon as possible. This is a place of entertainment, of social gathering, not the setting for some melodrama."

Ricky bristled, his face turning almost the same colour as his. "What are you saying lady?"

Okay, that was my cue to actually do something here. We wouldn't want this restaurant to fall to pieces simply because people couldn't communicate nicely. This whole situation was looking like it was going to get out of control, and instead of being in a nicely isolated warehouse, with the only potential injury being my own, we were in the middle of downtown Chicago, with many innocent, non-knowledgeable humans in the way. I stepped forward and put my hand on Dermot's shoulder, wearing my best charming smile and looking apologetically at the restaurant manager.

"You have our deepest apologies ma'am. We were meant to meet up later and the time simply slipped away. Of course, we shall leave immediately, just as soon as we've paid the check."

The mention of the check seemed to jolt the manager back to reality. She gave a tight nod and then snapped her fingers at one of the gaping waitstaff nearby, jerking her hand to indicate the three tables that our little group had accommodated, and then folding her arms stiffly. A few moments later, the waiter ran up to me, holding a chequebook with the receipt sticking out of the top, eyes wide and more than a little frightened. It occurred to me as I handed over the black credit card and signed the documents, that I wasn't at all scared. I didn't think it had anything to do with my lack of soul, my disconnect with my own emotions. Sure, my feelings were filtered through Al Capone and his experience with gunslingers is probably considerably more vast than my own, but this was, by far, one of the lesser dangerous situations I had been in. Yes, humans were potentially in the way, but I had a feeling if we could all control our tempers for a few more seconds, that this could be solved without a single injury. It would be chalked off to an unstable criminal element perhaps stepping out of bounds.

Once the card had been returned to me and everything squared away—I left large tips for the waiters—I clapped Dermot on the shoulder again and widened my smile. "Mr. Green, Mrs. Green, perhaps we should go rendezvous with our associates now."

Mathilde opened her mouth to say something, her eyes still flashing with anger, but Neja appeared at my left elbow and Agravane at my right, and she decided to keep her mouth shut. For now. Dermot looked at me with pleading wide eyes, but he did as I said. We all of us walked out of the restaurant without anything more but the glare from the restaurant manager, and found ourselves on the streets, the sky dark and the casual bystander mostly gone.

The van in which I had been taken earlier was parked at the curb, its lights flashing so that it wouldn't be ticketed in a loading only zone. All of the thugs besides Ricky and Dermot piled into the van, leaving Mathilde, Neja, Agravane and myself standing by as witnesses as Dermot and Ricky squared off.

They both looked as though they were about to say something, probably violent, when sirens sounded a couple blocks away. The restaurant manager has finally managed to dial the police. Risking my hide once again, I stepped between Ricky and Dermot.

"As much as I would like an explanation for this, perhaps we should do this somewhere else? It would be rather inconvenient to have to involve the police at this moment." Something about my tone of voice or my expression or whatever must have convinced both parties that I was deadly serious, because they both exchanged one more furious glare before traipsing off to the van. I turned to Mathilde, who was standing again with her arms crossed and her hip jutting out. "My sincerest apologies for this. I was unaware that tensions were this high. Perhaps if you would go back to your apartment, I could drop Dermot off when we are done?"

Mathilde scoffed, tossing her hair over her shoulder. "Not a chance. I'm in this now. I'm tired of being second to Dermot's work. If things are gonna work out between us, as you so oddly desire, then I'm going with you."

She stalked off, her heels clicking on the concrete. She opened the passenger side door in the front and sat in the chair, nose lifted. That left Neja, Agravane and myself, and I needed to be in the van within the next few seconds. Or they would leave us behind.

"Boss, maybe we should—"

"We're going. And you're coming with. Because I have a feeling this is not going to end well." With that, I turned and climbed into the van, which was getting rather full at this point. Agravane followed, his tall, well-built frame taking up more space. Neja peered into the back, frowned, then shook her head.

"You know what, I'll just meet up with you later."

Before I could say anything, Mathilde's voice cut through the air. "Get in the van, djinn."

Irritation flashed across Neja's features, her teeth sharpening into predatory points. A moment later and the terrifying desire was gone, replaced with the usual cool, snarky expression that I knew. She climbed daintily into the van, looking around for an empty seat. The only one left was the centre middle seat in the back row. Neja looked at the slightly intelligent thug. "You sit there, I'll sit next to Cal."

He did not argue for even an instant, just doing as he was ordered and saying not a word about it. Neja settled into the seat beside me and buckled in. She leaned in closer to me, giving me a wink and conspiratorially look. "I will say this about you, Cal, you sure know how to have a good time. I haven't had this much fun since I followed around a travelling circus of magical beings trafficking stolen antiquities."

"The sad thing is, I believe you. What's even worse than that, as this is turning out to be a fairly normal night for me."

Neja cackled and wrapped her arm around mine, patting it in comfort.

The van peeled away from the curb, Ricky's driving skills leaving something to be desired. We all went off to who knows where in silence, none of us ready to voice our thoughts until there was at least a modicum of privacy. That, and I think driving was making us all nauseous.

I was less than surprised when we pulled into a building that was adjacent to the warehouse I had been killed in earlier. This one was not empty, containing various boxes and equipment for some sort of factory work. It also had stairs to a second level, which was where Dermot led us, his hand in Mathilde's as they ascended the stairs. I couldn't tell if he was still acting for the sake of winning her over to free his finances, or if he truly had convinced himself that rekindling whatever it was he had with her was worthwhile. It didn't really matter to me, considering I just needed him to pay his back taxes, but part of me wanted them to end up together, to do well, to be happy. Most of me, though, knew that Life didn't like to work like that.

We all piled into the conference room, sitting around a very expensive wooden board room table and chairs, despite the slightly rickety feeling of the room. This must have been Dermot's centre of operations, the place where he had run his Mafia crime gang, up until preparing to sign the deal with the feds. So much for the microbrewery in the Taxman's files. It probably just had really good food and beer.

Dermot sank into the largest chair at the head of the table, steepling his fingers like some sort of furious villain. Ricky stood, his hands braced on the back of one of the chairs, his expression serious. "We have been trying to get in touch with you for days, boss. Do you even know what's been happening here? And then this guy, earlier, he was saying all sorts of stuff. He should be dead! What if you got yourself into? And when are you coming back?"

Dermot flicked me a look, something uncertain in the way that he held his shoulders. I raised my eyebrows, waiting for his explanation. If I leapt in now with some sort of story, no matter how rational, it would be taken very poorly. These people were concerned about Dermot, and he was ghosting them, preparing to run away. I didn't particularly like them, nor did I want them to survive another day to be criminals, but I didn't think that Dermot's plan was perhaps the best one. Then again, not many people had the stomach to act normally around those you knew would soon be arrested.

"Surely I have established our business well enough that it can run for several days without my input," Dermot said at last, his voice harder than I had expected. "Surely you don't need to come running to me every time someone moves a drop half a foot or pays in euros instead of dollars? Surely you don't need to interrupt my date night with my wife in order to reassure yourselves that the world is not falling to pieces?! Or are you that incompetent?"

Dermot was shouting at the end, his words falling off as Ricky stared at him wide-eyed. I moved to say something, and felt Al's hand on my arm, slightly incorporeal and yet solid enough that I could feel him. Another perk of our connection through a shared soul, I imagined. He shook his head, his eyes solemn and his scar shining in the florescent light.

"Trust me, this is not something that you want to step into lightly. These things run on hierarchy, on capability. And even if he is leaving the life, he hasn't done so yet. He is still in charge. And until he has signed those papers and walked away, then he needs to demand respect from his people. Or he won't be walking away at all, but will either be shackled here forever, or end up very dead." To my surprise, Al was deeply serious. I felt none of his usual smugness or arrogance through our connection, and what emotions did bubble to the surface were more along the lines of resignation and perhaps even a little guilt. And layers upon layers of anger.

In this, I trusted his knowledge more than my own. I settled back in my seat and watched as Dermot and Ricky stared each other down.

Finally, Ricky moved back from the chair, holding up his hands. He sat and leaned his elbows on the table. "Look, boss, things can run for days without your input, but me and the boys are just so used to having you around, we got worried when you didn't show up. Especially with that shipment of dragonwort coming in from the goblins. You know they don't like dealing with anyone but you, and they was awful nervous when you didn't show up."

"Am I not allowed to spend time with my wife? Am I not allowed to take a few days off to plan how to woo her, to make things better between us? You were insolent to think that you could come to the restaurant and demand my attention. You are not another leader, nor are you a Lord in your own right. You are my vassal, *my servant*, pledged to me. I see that you have forgotten such things after spending so much time in the mortal realms." Dermot lifted one side of his mouth in a ferocious smile, displaying for the first time since I had met him the sort of malicious cunning that one needed to run a criminal empire. He was not as overtly powerful as some beings that I had met, but nor was he insignificant. He was smart and he was capable, and he had perhaps more ability than many humans, setting him up here as something to be feared.

For the first time, I understood it.

"Perhaps," Dermot said slowly, leaning forward until he was facing down Ricky like a wolf, "you need to be sent back to Elsewhere, to learn precisely what place you hold in the grand scheme of things."

Ricky paled and shrank into himself. He lowered his gaze and stared at his hands. "No, it's okay. I understand my place. I made a mistake and I apologise. Whatever reparations you see fit I shall pay."

Dermot leaned back in his chair, looking at all of us around the table. Neja, Agravane and myself had said nothing, and the other thugs were obviously too cowed to say anything either. Mathilde was watching with interest, her eyes flicking between Ricky and Dermot as she sized up the power difference between them. Once, her eyes even flicked to me, though they moved away before I can read any significance in the glance. Obviously our confrontation at the restaurant had not been forgotten.

"You shall begin by apologising to my wife for ruining our evening. And then, you are going to go and see that everything is running smoothly. I don't care if you have to walk from dealer to dealer, I want to make sure that every person in my organisation knows what their place is, and knows what they are doing. I will expect a full report by dawn."

As far as punishments went, that seemed fairly tame, though I didn't know how many dealers or employees Dermot's organisation had. Nor did I know what they were dealing—he had said dragonwort, but I didn't know what that was. I would have to ask Agravane.

I did know that I wanted this organisation taken down. I was tired of a world built on hierarchy, where power and violence was used as currency instead of mutual respect and understanding. I knew full well that this was how the world worked, especially amongst Elsewhere, but maybe was just because I was a little guy, I wanted something different. I had stood up to Life and Death and struggled through. I wanted the same chance for others. Not to mention, I did not want Ricky running this organisation. Maybe the feds would be able to take him down. Maybe they wouldn't. I didn't know, but I would lend my assistance as best I could manage.

Ricky bowed his head, like a dog showing its belly to its alpha. He turned to Mathilde and lowered himself further, sinking to his knees on the floor. "You have my sincerest apologies for ruining your pleasant evening, my great lady."

Mathilde let out a scream, her voice lending in a double timbre, tones of fury overlaid with that strange reverberating sound that rattled your bones. She closed her mouth a moment later, her banshee powers gone. Everyone in the room was visibly shaken except for Agravane and Neja. I pulled off my glasses and cleaned them, forcing myself to keep a calm expression. Ricky was trembling on the floor.

"Don't you forget, little red cap that Dermot did not marry me simply because of my looks." Mathilde smiled, the expression as fake as her hair colour. Ricky did not seem to notice. He just held up his hands and nodded several times. The other thugs shifted uncomfortably in their chairs. Ricky started to stand, still trembling, when, once again we were interrupted.

This time, it was the feds. I guess they really didn't want to wait until tomorrow.

TAX LAW

They came swarming into the room like mice, about six or so of them, all decked out in their body armour and guns. I wasn't really a gun person. It seemed rather silly to have so many of them floating around, but this room had suddenly become the epitome of what I considered to be folly. The feds had their guns pointed at Dermot and his people—of which I apparently was one—and the mafia types had their guns pointed at the feds. Really, there should have been a much more civilised way of going about things.

After much shouting and noise, things eventually quieted down enough to the point where the thugs had lowered their weapons, the feds had moved their fingers off the triggers, and what I assumed was the leader of the group had walked in. She at least looked like someone who knew how to be civilised. She was tall and perhaps in her fifties, her hair slate grey and neatly cut at her shoulders. She did not seem to care one way or another whether she showed wrinkles or age, though her features were fairly smooth for someone who held such a fierce scowl. She, too, wore body armour, but she also had sensible business attire underneath it. Her slacks were tucked into the tops of high laced combat boots, shining and black. And her gun was holstered, a concession to the fact that she was an American federal officer and had to carry such things.

She would have made an excellent denizen of Elsewhere, but as far as I could tell, she was perfectly, ordinarily, human.

She was terrifying, and I admired her. The contradiction did confuse me for a moment, before I realised that most of the terror was coming from Al, as well as a good deal of the admiration.

"Now there is a worthy opponent," Al said. I fought the urge to make a face at him, instead doing my best to remain calm so that none of the newcomers would shoot me and discover my particular skill set. I really, really didn't want to be experimented on. Not that I was certain the American government did such things, but since this whole situation seems to be moving in the direction of a melodramatic soap opera, as Agravane had hoped, I couldn't be too sure.

"My apologies for the intrusion, but we received a complaint about a disturbance at a downtown restaurant, and you missed our meeting Mr. Green." The woman strode towards Dermot, completely unfazed by his stance of power. Ricky, still cowering on the floor or from where he had been apologising to Mathilde, lifted his head and narrowed his eyes. For once, he displayed a modicum of intelligence and said nothing.

"Agent Ferris. I do hope that you and your people opened the door rather than breaking it down. It was left unlocked." Dermot sounded bored by the whole situation. Judging by the way his hands were still held above his head, I very much doubted that it was really what was going on inside his head.

Agent Ferris tilted her head and gave a little smile. "Oops."

"Do you have probable cause for entering this warehouse?" Dermot asked, a little bit of tension creeping into his posture. Agent Ferris blinked languidly and then turned on her heel to point at me.

"A street camera caught sight of your associates kidnapping this man and bringing him here. Unfortunately, it took rather longer than we expected to call up the search warrant. But we're here now. Sir, could you point out your kidnappers to me?" Ferris fixed me with a ruthless smile, perhaps thinking that she had me in some sort of trap.

"I'm afraid I don't know what you're talking about. I am here on behalf of the IRS to discuss the nature of these gentlemen's taxes. There are some discrepancies in the business records that we would like straightened out." I returned her expression with a wide smile of my own, trying not to look as vicious as Al beside me. I don't think my innocent bystander act went over very well. Ferris frowned.

"The IRS. Really?" Several of the agents still holding guns on Dermot and his people looked uncertainly at their boss. Ferris stepped forward, watching me as though she could tell whether or not I was telling the truth just by looking.

"Yes, yes, I know. I'm the last sort that you would expect working for the American tax service, being from across the pond and all, but it turns out that they'll hire you if you're qualified. If you are uncertain about such things, then you are welcome to check my identification, which is in my jacket pocket." I had barely finished getting my words out before Ferris surged forward with the grace of a well-trained panther, her hand darting into my jacket pocket and pulling out the badge that the Taxman had given me in the packet of information. I was glad that I had carried it around, because that would have been very awkward otherwise.

"Calvin Thorpe, IRS. Sent from DC." Ferris lifted her eyes to look at me, narrowing them. She sniffed and handed me back my badge. I put it away, lowering my arms.

There was a lull, as Ferris thought about what to do next. Obviously, the search warrant had allowed her access to his building, but she couldn't do very much now that I had quashed her plans. And if she wanted to meet Dermot and me tomorrow regarding my involvement, then there was really no need for her to be there. I was just an innocent government worker, caught up in a situation far beyond my purview.

"Mr. Green," Ferris said, snapping her head to stare at Dermot, "perhaps you could accompany me to my office and explain precisely why it is that the Chicago police received a telephone call about a disturbance involving you, this gentleman, and several of…your people at a well respected restaurant this evening."

Dermot scoffed, shaking his head and looking at his people. "Do I have a choice?"

Ferris smiled wanly. "No. You do not."

For the sake of his employees, Dermot rolled his eyes loudly. Then, he put his arms down and made a show of straightening out his dinner jacket and adjusting his bow tie. Then, with an arrogant tilted his head, he walked towards Ferris, unafraid and unapologetic. I heard several of the thugs snorting in appreciation.

"Don't worry, boss," Ricky said, scrambling to his feet and dusting himself off. "We'll call a lawyer and get you out of there right away."

Ferris snorted, shaking her head. She turned and waved to her people. "Come along. Back to the office. Oh, and Mr. Thorpe, if you could come with us as well, I would be very curious to hear precisely what discrepancies the IRS has found with Mr. Dermot's business."

"Very well," I said. I gestured to Agravane, who was watching Ferris as though she were another predator, equally dangerous as him and encroaching on his territory. It was a look I hadn't seen from him since before our escape from the Order of Silence. "My business associate and I shall be glad to accompany you. Agent Ferris, this is Agravane…Mort. He works with me and knows just a much about Mr. Green's account as I do."

Agravane shook himself, his wary expression floating away as though he had called a breeze in.

Ferris narrowed her eyes. "It is a pleasure to be at your service, Agent Ferris," Agravane said with a flourish, his predatory gleam still very much present. Ferris raised her brows and studied him for a moment before shrugging and walking out the door. As one, her people followed her, not even questioning whether or not Dermot, Agravane, or myself were coming with them. We just did precisely as was expected and walked out into the night, only to be faced with another van ride back into the centre of the city.

"Why does it smell like peanuts?" I whispered to Agravane. He shifted his gaze to me, his dark glower turning into a startled look. I eyed him pointedly. Agravane nodded, forcing his shoulders to relax.

"I think you're mistaken, Cal. It distinctly smells like Chinese take away." With that, I was certain that he would be all right, that whatever this was would come second to what was most important right then. That of course being getting Dermot out of this in one piece so that he could get Mathilde to sign the papers releasing their funds and pay the back taxes. At which point, I could go home and the closest thing I would ever come to this sort of situation again would be whatever television show Yolanda and Agravane forced on me next.

I looked out the window as the van pulled away and saw Neja standing in the street behind us, her eyes shining like lights in the dark. I didn't know what it meant, but it sent shivers down my spine. I turned back away from the window and settled in for another awful drive.

I wondered, since I had seen Neja appear almost out

of thin air as we started our drive, if her wish magic would do its best to kill me again. I was tense the whole drive to the federal building, wondering if I would have to push these people out of the van before they got caught up in the backwash of wish magic.

Agravane was right. I needed to learn how to defend myself from such things, even if it was only for the sake of preventing others from getting caught up in my own ridiculous reality. Thankfully, though, nothing happened during the drive to the building, nor did anything happen upon exiting the end traipsing into the building by the parking garage. It looked as though I would be allowed to have a nice, relatively relaxing conversation.

Ferris send a glare in my direction, hidden behind layers of stoicism. Oh yes, this was going to be terribly relaxing.

Compared to the IRS building, this building, home to the local FBI branch, was both far more organised and far less organised. The agents all had cubicles and desks made out of flimsy materials, stacked with papers and arranged in such a way that people could move easily between them. At this time of night, there weren't a whole lot of people there, which made the building feel empty and ominous.

I hadn't learned much about ghosts since working for Death—though now that seems a little ironic—but I had a feeling that this building had many ghosts. And judging by the way that Ferris's shoulders settled under some unknowable weight, I had a feeling that a lot of the ghosts haunted her.

"Be careful Cal," Al whispered, his own shoulders hunched in his eyes darting around nervously. "These people might not want to let you leave."

"I work for the Taxman," I breathed, making sure that I kept my voice quiet enough so that only Al could hear. I don't know why it was even bothering to respond. But something in me way that he spoke, the wary tone in his voice with emotion that surged upwards through his soul and into me, had me pushing myself to comfort him. "These people can do nothing to me. And even if they try, then there are other resources I can call upon."

Al's shoulders settled and he nodded. I don't know what sort of meaning he took from my statement, but if he thought that I would call Death upon this building just to get out of here without being accosted by bureaucrats and agents with guns, then he was sorely mistaken. Still, it seemed to make him feel better, so I let the matter lie.

The agents that had escorted us, their guns very obviously out and pointing in our direction, peeled off one by one until only Agent Ferris was left, escorting us to the conference room. It was about the same setup and quality of the conference room and Dermot's warehouse and I swallowed a chuckle, deciding that it would probably be wise not to draw attention to that similarity. Neither party would appreciate it.

"Please, have a seat, gentlemen." Ferris swept her hand to indicate the conference table. Agravane looked at me out of the corner of his eye and I nodded. We both sat, settling into our chairs and doing our best to look professional, at ease. After all, we were theoretically part of the same system that Ferris was. In actuality, nothing could be further from the truth. "Can I get you something to drink? Some bottled water?"

"Please," I said. Ferris eyed me for a moment, the slightest twitch suggesting that she rather wanted me to refuse, that she wanted me uncomfortable and off balance. She had certainly succeeded in that with Dermot, who was sitting quietly in his chair, the most domicile I had seen him yet. Ferris strode from the room, returning a few moments later with bottles of water, which she slid across the table to us.

She sat. Placed her hands on the table looking benevolent, the kindly matron just warning us to cooperate and confess to our sins. Well, at least that was the image I imagine she was trying to portray. Instead, it was like looking at the steel eyed prison warden.

"Well Dermot? What do you have to say for yourself? We were promised daily check ins, as well as the assurance that you would not be making contact with your people. You should have told us about this situation with these...IRS agents." Ferris didn't look at Agravane or myself, just stared Dermot down. The fetch swallowed, his image wobbling for a moment, taking on the shadow and appearance of the woman sitting across from him. I coughed pointedly and his doppelgänger shift faded.

"Interesting," Ferris said. "Is there a particular reason why you are trying to get Mr. Green to keep silent, Mr. Thorpe?"

I opened a bottle of water, taking a healthy sip. "I

don't know what you mean. I was just thirsty. It turns out that I am adversely affected by stressful situations."

Agravane snorted, unable to hide the amusement. Ferris snapped her attention to him, tilting her head like a raptor searching out prey. It didn't work as far as intimidation tactics went. Agravane was an aurai, a powerful magical being, and one who had seen the darker side of things. His arrogance would cost us.

"And you," Ferris said smoothly. "Why would a tax auditor be sent here with someone like you? You are obviously not a tax accountant."

Agravane raised his brows, flushing some of that charm at Ferris. I tried not to wince. "Why would you say that? I am perfectly capable at accounting. Balance sheets are like candy."

Agravane, you idiot.

"Indeed? Then you won't mind my asking what university you attended to get your degree? After all, a simple background check would make this whole situation so much easier. We wouldn't have to be assuming the worst about each other," Ferris said. Yep. She was not one to be underestimated. Agravane's charms might have worked well on creatures from Elsewhere, and in the marketing world smiles worked a fair bit, but here? It required a different sort of persuasiveness.

"What is it exactly that you suspect us of?" I asked, leaning forward and putting on a quizzical expression.

"Did you know that Dermot here was going into the witness protection program?" Ferris asked. Dermot winced, but I just shrugged.

"Of course I did. It was some of the paperwork that

went through that got the attention of my department. There are certain financial laws and transactions that go into effect when a potential witness goes into the program. Some of that includes, hmm, difficulties with the repayment of large sums of back taxes. As it is, Mr. Green owes nearly 1.8 million dollars in back taxes, and we are very keen to collect." Just for good measure, I pushed my glasses up my nose. Ferris looked at me in disbelief.

"You honestly expect me to believe that you, someone like you, truly works for the IRS? Not only is there the matter of your heritage —"

I sniffed in disdain. "Do you have something against people from England? I will have you know that I got my MBA from Harvard, my degree in tax law from Boston University. Simply because I happened to be born and raised in one of the world's most civilised countries does not mean that I am incapable of working for the American government. Besides, if it makes you feel better, my mother was an American citizen."

Lies, lies, lies. Well, mostly.

Ferris gaped at me for a moment, then shook herself and I was once again faced with the stoic law keeper. "Since when do tax agents wear tailored suits? Since when do they wear silk ties imported from Italy? Since when did they walk around with glasses as beat up as yours. Do you know what I think? I think you represent people who are interested in acquiring Dermot's business before he disappears from view. I think you know that he's going to go into wit sec and that you are doing all you can to protect your new assets. Hiding money are we Dermot? How much are they paying you?"

Before Dermot could open his mouth and say something that would perhaps completely ruin everything, I straightened in my chair, bristling indignantly for all it was worth. "How dare you! You have seen my identification. Surely you must be aware of the discrepancies in Mr. Green's business reporting. A federal agent such as yourself would not make such a deal without knowing all of the information first. All I am trying to do is see that the government is paid what they are due. And here you are, accusing me of colluding with the criminal empire."

Ferris sneered, wrinkling her nose at me. "I don't trust you. I don't trust anyone who hasn't been verified and triple checked. Until that happens, I shall hold you in the highest suspicion. Whether you like it or not, Dermot Green is going to go into the witness protection program starting on Saturday. If you haven't gotten your money by then, that is not my problem."

"That, madam, is all that I am trying to accomplish. If it so please you, you are free to join my associate Agravane and I for breakfast at our hotel. We shall provide you with all of the documentation that you demand." With that, I huffed, stood, dusted off my jacket as best I could, and strode to the door. Agravane followed suit, his posture perhaps a little too casual his smile a little too glib, but the effects generally what I was hoping for. Dermot stared after us, eyes wide. I gave him a significant look and then turned to Ferris, who was watching us with predatory stillness.

"And my glasses are broken because they fell on the ground and were crushed. It's rather hard to get same day prescription glasses repaired when you live somewhere else. My spare pair is back home. So thank you, for judging me based on my looks. It's nice to know that the FBI has evolved to such standards."

I walked from the room, not waiting for a response. As soon as the door shut behind me, I knew I had taken a step too far. And I knew that it hadn't come entirely from me. Al Capone was snickering, his mirth easily visible. I stared at him until he caught my eye, and all he had the nerve to do was offer a shrug. "Serves her right. Serves this whole agency right. When I get into my own again, things will change."

Not if I had anything to do with it.

Agravane and I made it almost out of the building before Agent Ferris stopped us. She was walking swiftly up behind us from the elevator bay, her expression is cold, as ever, seemingly perfectly unruffled, as if she were running into us casually at a café. Dermot was nowhere to be seen.

"Mr. Thorpe, Mr. Mort, just a moment if you please." Ferris strode up to us, her legs eating up the floor and reminding me of a prowling cat. I paused, putting my hands and my pockets, and Agravane did the same. Ferris smiled, the polite expression sharper than it should've been. "I just thought that I would offer you a ride back to your hotel."

I waited a heartbeat, wondering precisely how I should answer after all the accusations she had thrown at us. "Where is Mr. Green? Surely you have business with him to attend to."

"Dermot is filling out some paperwork for the future change in his circumstances. Afterwards, he will be escorted back to his apartment. You have my assurances that he will be safe." Ferris put a hand to her heart, as though that were my concern. It was, partly, but there was more to it than that. Behind me, Agravane shifted, and I could feel his unease.

Or maybe that was Al's unease, floating up through our connection.

"There is really no need for a personal escort back to our hotel. After all, there is this wonderful technology called ride sharing. I pulled out my phone and waved it before Ferris, watching as her eyes tracked the technology. She blinked and that polite smile was back.

"It's really no trouble. Besides, it will save you a few dollars and you will not have to worry about dealing with people so late at night on the streets of Chicago."

I was beginning to get the impression this we didn't have much of a choice. It wasn't as though Ferris could actually do Agravane or myself any harm. One way or another, we would no longer be in the mortal realms come Saturday. She had no leverage on us apart from our current task, and we hadn't committed any crimes. Since I didn't really feel like arguing, I decided to accept. Though I didn't want her to think that I had given it so easily.

I stifled a bored yawn. "You make your city sound dangerous. Perhaps not the impression that you wish to give to visitors." Anger flashed across her features for a moment and she looked as though she was going to say something. I held up my hands. "But, since you insist, I will not protest to a ride."

Al mated noise of displeasure, his form moving

closer to me as he glared over my shoulder at Ferris. I slammed him down with my will, not really wanting to deal with his personal vendetta at the moment. I held my arm out, indicating the exit, and Ferris led the way, her mouth twisted in displeasure. Agravane followed behind me, starting to whistle. I was really far too tired for this, but at the end of this ride would be a bed with some of the best mattress and sheets waiting for me.

We were led into the parking garage without another word between us, the humid Chicago air smelling like must despite its heat. It was well after dark, edging on towards eleven, midnight, I wasn't sure which. But even in the theoretical coolness of night, the air was sweltering. And that was just in the parking garage. I resisted the urge to undo my tie, to unbutton my shirt collar. I knew the power of appearances just as well as Agent Ferris, for an entirely different reason. There was no cause for her to know that I was uncomfortable in any way.

"Cal, are you sure this is a good idea?" Agravane whispered in my ear as we approached one of the government vehicles. I looked at him, a little surprised, and found him watching Ferris approach her car with that same predatory look and gait. If I didn't know better, I would assume that she was walking with preternatural ability rather than human grace. Apparently, such a thing made Agravane, as much a predator as anyone, uncomfortable. I patted him on the arm, the gesture not as reassuring as I would've liked.

"It's a short ride to the hotel. Surely things will be fine." Before Agravane could voice another protest, I stepped around to the passenger door of the car and slid into the seat. Agravane followed, sliding into the back and putting on his seatbelt with an ominous click. Ferris waited until I had done the same before starting the engine, pulling back and driving out of the parking garage with a squeal of tires.

"Where are you staying?" she asked. I told her. She pulled her attention from the road and raised her eyebrows at me, obviously shocked. I scowled.

"There was a mixup. By the time I learned of it, it was too late. I'm going to be taking this particular mixup out of my assistant's pay." I wouldn't, really, but I was still very annoyed at the cost. Neja's reassurances hadn't been all that reassuring, nor had anyone else's. Death might be wealthy—in fact he probably was—but this whole expedition had cost me far more than I liked and I was going to make Agravane collate every single receipt when we got back.

Ferris laughed. The sound was so startling that I broke out of my musings on receipts and expense sheets to gape at her. The laugh was genuine. And more than that it was deep, creating lines on her face where there had been none before. That in itself surprised me. She did not strike me as a person who laughed often, and yet the lines were evidence to that fact.

"I might have been mistaken about you. No gangster or mafia man or whatever would be quite so concerned about a mistaken hotel booking." Ferris chuckled again, shaking her head as she turned down a different street.

"I assure you, we are here simply for the reason of

back taxes. I was not assigned this case by choice, but I am going to see it through." I continued to watch the FBI agent more than the streets, gauging her reaction. She shrugged.

"I want to believe you. I admire your spunk," she said. "I could even like you. However, your timing is extremely suspect. As is the fact that you know about Mr. Green's upcoming entrance into wit sec." We stopped at a red light, Ferris's eyes flicking to me for half a second before returning to the road. Agravane shuffled in the seat behind us, and I swore that I heard a quiet growl arising from his throat.

"I was only assigned the case a few days ago," I said, figuring that a small truth wouldn't really hurt things. "When I arrived out here and spoke with Mr. Green, I learned the particular difficulties surrounding his case. I believe he told me about the witness protection program simply because I am from a fellow govern-ment agency. Not to mention that he needed my help in releasing the funds so that he could pay the taxes."

Which reminded me that things were far from resolved. Tomorrow was going to involve a good deal of damage control.

So much for sleeping in.

"That explains why you were at the restaurant. You're trying to help Dermot patch things up with his crazy wife so that you can get the funds released and have the taxes paid. I've heard saner plans in my day." There it went again, that laugh. This time, it was directed at me. I scowled deeper.

"All I want is the taxes paid. If that means that I have

to play Cupid, then I will." I lifted my chin, turning my attention outside the window so that I wouldn't have to see the reaction flit across Ferris's features, though I could guess what it was. Agravane was also chuckling, though his was dry, wary.

Whatever agent Ferris was going to say in response to that, I didn't hear it. As I glanced out the window, my attention was flagged by the traffic light post. It was swaying, as if in a storm. Only, there was no storm. There was no one else around, and we had already been at that light longer than I would have expected.

The light changed.

Ferris started inching the car forwards.

My heart beat my ears. Once. Twice.

The traffic light started to fall, the metal groaning under magical stress. Neja's wish magic was coming for me, as I had expected it would, and an innocent was going to get in the way.

"Agravane!" I screamed, lunging for the wheel and wrenching it, fighting Ferris every moment. I don't know what I expected Agravane to do, but he took my warning at face value, throwing open the car door and leaping out mid motion. The car spun, Ferris losing control as it accelerated and the traffic light fell. Everything seemed to be happening in slow motion. I had enough time, therefore, to realise that my plans for getting her out of the way were going to come to naught. I couldn't move fast enough. I would come back from death, she would not.

I unbuckled my seatbelt, shoving out of my seat with one leg braced against the car door, lunging for

Ferris. Her eyes wide, she turned in her seat, one hand reaching for her holstered gun. The gun was pulled half way out of the holster by the time I wriggled myself out of my seat far enough to throw the body over top of hers, pinning her beneath me even as the metal of the traffic light screamed and swung onto the car, crushing the roof and, by consequence, me.

Something broke in my back, the pressure from the traffic light buckling my spine. There was a roar of pain, then nothing, and then that familiar whiteness. My death reversed, as it had done so many times before, but this time was different. This time, there was a human body pinned beneath me, a person still living, her eyes wide, terrified, arms trapped is she had tried to cover her head. I sucked in a breath, my arm muscles trembling as I tried to hold myself up for enough that I wouldn't crush her.

"Are you okay?" I managed as I ground my teeth together, pain still sprouting all over my body. The fatal wound to my spine had been healed, but there was something jabbed into the back of my left calf, another something piercing my right shoulder. The pain was enough to almost make me blank out again. I sucked in a breath, smelling acrid smoke and the tang of metal.

"You…How…?" Ferris managed, her breath coming in short and sharp. I was struggling to come up with an answer that would explain a question that hadn't even been asked when Agravane pulled something open and released fresh muggy air into the car.

"Come on, this way." Agravane held out a hand to Ferris, who looked at it for a moment before reaching out and taking it, her own hand shaking almost uncontrollably. Shock. Agravane pulled her out through the car, some of that magical power probably doing him a great deal of good right then. I was more than thankful for it. As soon as Ferris was out of the car and on the ground, her legs too unstable for her to stand, Agravane reached in and pulled me out. My body and all of its unhealed injuries protested. Loudly.

"If we don't get Neja to put an end to this wish magic soon..." Agravane trailed off, his voice falling into silence and eyes serious. I nodded in agreement, yelping when he reached out and pulled a jagged piece of car from my shoulder. Not a fatal wound, as I didn't black out and the pain remained, throbbing and time with my anxiety.

"Yeah," I said. "It's getting more dramatic. It's getting worse. Innocent people are starting to get caught up in this, too."

Agravane nodded, his expression bearing some of that same glistening desperation that he had worn when I first found him, pinned to a rock. Things were bad. And judging by the reaction of the FBI agents now on the ground, doing her best to control her breathing, I had a feeling things were only going to get worse.

"Prepare yourself for a long night," I said as Agravane slung my good arm around his shoulders so that I could stagger further away from the wreck. "I doubt either of us is going to be getting much sleep until this is done."

So much for my lovely dreams of that bed in the hotel.

Someone had obviously witnessed the crash, because a few minutes later the paramedics seemed to magically appear in the intersection, their lights blazing and giving me a splitting headache. For the second time that day, I sat in the back of an ambulance, trying to downplay my injuries. This time, though, they didn't quite believe me. After pulling out metal from my calf, seeing massive amounts of bruising on my back, and putting large amounts of gauze on my shoulder, the paramedics practically demanded that I go to the hospital. I refused, just as adamantly.

I wasn't going to let sick and injured people come anywhere near me, in case the wish magic acted again and others were hurt. Finally, since they couldn't actually force me to go to the hospital, they relented, patching me up as best they could in the back of the ambulance and then driving away. Thankfully, they took Agent Ferris with them, her trembling hands and her breathing bad enough that she didn't dare refuse. Not that I think she was thinking straight, either. As they loaded her into the back of the ambulance, I saw her eyes tracking me, wide and shining as though with admiration or fear.

"You have to get off the street." This piece of blatantly obvious advice came from Al, his eyes were taking in my injury and also the looks of the bystanders who had come to gawk at the mess. "You're vulnerable here."

"No. They are vulnerable here." I jerked my head at the bystanders, with the city buildings standing above them. If one of them came down as Neja's magic intensified, then who knows how many people would be on my conscience. I turned to Agravane, stumbling away from the scene of the latest incident. "I need to find a place to stay the night, far away from other people. And if you can get Neja there too, and maybe we can sort this thing out."

Before I even finished speaking, Agravane pulled out his phone and was dialling furiously, turning his back on me so he could converse, saying things in an unfamiliar language and waving his hands. He paced, his voice getting increasingly louder until it cut off. There were a few whispered words, and then Agravane hung up his phone. I limped towards him.

"We're going back to Dermot's warehouse. Neja will meet us there." Agravane looked down at his phone, ordering a ride share for us to take. Sleeping at the warehouse—because no matter how serious the situation was, I could feel my body fairly trembling from all of the things I had put it through today—was going to be no picnic compared to the hotel that I had dreamed about, but it would keep other people from getting hurt. I could hardly complain about that.

And as soon as Neja got there, we were going to sort this out.

TAX INCLUDED

By the time Neja met us at the warehouse, Agravane and I had turned the conference room into a temporary living situation. That is, Agravane was sprawled out on the floor with some chair cushions as a mattress and I was standing at the window, watching the sky. It started raining, which did nothing to help the mugginess, but was probably very well received.

Neja startled me out of my watching the rain, trying not to pay attention to Al or to Agravane, who was now snoring. Al, at least, had settled onto a chair and was simply sitting, his arms folded, his expression thoughtful.

"I would have thought you would be sleeping with all that you've been through today," Neja said, the question more of a laughing statement than a request for information. I shrugged and turned away from the window, leaning against the sill. Neja was wearing the same jumpsuit as earlier, her white hair tied back, her silvery eyes flashing with the spark of some sort of fire. She looked just as she had when I met her, and yet she was different, now. A known entity. And still extremely mysterious besides.

"Why is it that I seem to trust you after knowing you for less than a day? Especially given the fact that your wish magic has done its best to kill me three times now. Yet, despite your attempt to look dangerous, and the fact that you are a bounty hunter for Elsewhere, and a private investigator besides, I don't think you actually mean me harm." I folded my arms, watching her reaction. What I got was perhaps one of the more genuine smiles I had seen from her. There was none of the arrogance, none of the ownership of the room simply by stepping in it, none of the swagger. Just quiet assurance and the knowledge that she was precisely who she meant to be and that while she didn't need to explain herself to me, I was perhaps figuring her out.

"You hired me," was all she said. I scoffed and shook my head, turning around staring out of the window once more, watching the city in the distance, its lights impossibly bright against the rain.

"I'm not sleeping because I don't have the same needs as Agravane. For all that he is aurai, highly trained and full of freedom, he is..." I couldn't quite bring myself to say the word.

"Mortal?" Neja stood at the window beside me, though I got the impression she wasn't actually looking at the scenery. "As much time as those of us who are truly immortal have, I would suggest that now is not the moment for musing on the nature of the world.

After all, you called me here for a reason. And I doubt it was just to talk. Though," Neja purred, moving a touch closer and sending shivers up my spine, "I do find you intriguing. Perhaps when all this is over."

I smiled, the motion feeling harder than it should have. "Perhaps. Though something tells me that as much as I might like to get involved with you, I should exercise some semblance of caution."

Neja nodded, then threaded her arm through mine. "Some, yes. But not too much."

Oh, to be able to live in that moment, to enjoy the company of a beautiful woman. I knew full well that time was fleeting and that I had to grasp onto everything that I could when I heard, they had to make the most of the moments that were presented to me, but as Neja had said, this was not that time.

I pulled away from her, trapping her hand in mine and bowing over it for a moment, the odd act of chivalry startling even me until I caught Al's smile out of the corner of my eye. Neja's grey blue skin darkened a touch at the cheek, and I said nothing about the blush. There were better times for this, Cal. I went over to Agravane and nudged him with my foot. In true style, he leapt to his feet and had me on my back with a flurry of limbs, before I could ask him to stop.

"Wake up," I wheezed. "Neja is here."

Agravane took a step back and gave me a sheepish smile, though he did not apologise. Not that I expected him to. "Once we actually get a chance to give you some proper training, maybe I won't be able to get the best of you."

"Great plan, wrong time." I coughed again, then climbed to my feet, feeling a little more tired than I had let on. I was more resilient to such things as exhaustion and hunger and thirst, but I still didn't do well without enough. This day had pushed me to some sort of limit and I could practically feel the bags under my eyes multiplying. Not to mention my injuries were still throbbing.

"So, why did you call me here?" Neja asked, though I had a feeling she already knew the answer.

"Your wish magic. The one that's trying to kill me? It's getting worse. An innocent person was almost killed today because of it," I said.

"One less contentious FBI agent in the world," Al said, ignoring my glare. "I will weep for her."

Neja closed her eyes and let out a long breath before going over to the table and sinking into one of the chairs. I sat in another one and Agravane took the one where Al was sitting, causing the gangster to rise from his chair, spluttering.

"That's the thing about wish fulfilment, it wants immediate results, instant gratification. If it didn't, then it wouldn't be wish magic. The longer it takes to achieve those results, the less subtle it is going to be about achieving its aim. I'm sorry, Cal, but unless we get Mathilde to rescind the wish, then the only other way to counter it is to wish it gone." Neja looked a little nervous, little uncomfortable. Thank goodness Agravane voiced my question before I could make myself sound even more ignorant than I knew I already was.

"You make it sound like it's a separate entity, like

you have no control over how you're aiming it." Agravane frowned and leaned back in his chair, assessing her. I couldn't tell if he was doing that from a predatory stance, from one which the Order of Silence would approve, or from a marketing stance, where having more information in order to portray a client's image, brand, whatever you want to call it, in the best light was key. The part that was disconcerting was that it did not bother me not knowing. I wanted both. And I think Agravane did too.

"Djinns are born from the confluence of magic and fire and desire. We are made from a wish. Some say that we are demons, some that we are benevolent, but the magic that we possess...We do not have control over it. It is wild, untamed. Perhaps not a separate entity, but an alien one? With motivations not even we can decipher. That's why it requires rituals to use it, and precision to execute it. It's beyond dangerous." Neja's eyes bored into the table, and I could almost feel the heat rising from them, like a fire sparking and crackling at wet wood.

"If it were just me getting caught up in this, then I wouldn't bother. But it's not anymore. Innocent people are getting tangled in this, and I can't have them losing their lives over me." I waited until Neja lifted her gaze to stare at me, and then I held it, hoping to press my point home. Instead, she frowned.

"They would not be losing their lives over you, they would be losing them because Mathilde made a mistake and couldn't control her wish properly. It is not your doing."

I nodded. Sat back. Took a breath. This was the reason why so many people in Elsewhere had a hard time understanding me. I was human, not magical, not supernatural, not Elsewhere, just human. And humans thought differently about things. They didn't have the powers of the universe at their disposal. But we were stubborn and vivacious and so very good at life. Perhaps that made us stupid, but it was also our one great advantage. And for me, having more power at my disposal than most, it made me responsible for others who got hurt because of me.

"Maybe it is, maybe it isn't," was the best answer I could give. "What about getting Mathilde to resend the wish?"

Neja shook her head. "I talked to her about it when I went over earlier this afternoon. Unless we go through the ritual again, perform another wish ceremony, it can't just be rescinded. We tried. She can't afford another wish ceremony."

I didn't say anything for a moment, wondering why it was that she was only mentioning this to me now. Just because I couldn't I didn't mean I wanted to be followed around by wish magic until I went back to elsewhere. I looked up from staring outside the window and focus my attention on Neja, watching her expression to see if it would give me a clue as to an answer. Her denial seemed too simple, too easy, just given at the wrong time. Maybe it was just my experience talking, but I didn't trust it. As much as I wanted to trust her.

"I didn't tell you earlier, Cal, because there was

nothing I could do without enacting another wish. That is…That is beyond dangerous. I don't think you understand *how* dangerous. Napoleon was one of the last human leaders to get his hands on wish magic. Look how that turned out." Neja shrugged, as if it were out of her power.

Did she not understand? People were getting hurt. This wasn't just a matter of waiting until I was gone and the magic was forced to dissipate because of the boundaries between the moral realms and Elsewhere. This needed to end. I couldn't even do my job and get Dermot and Mathilde to sort things out unless this ended.

"Didn't you think this was something I should know?" I asked quietly. Neja sucked in a breath and wrapped her arms around her waist. It was vulnerable look for a creature that was far from vulnerable. I wanted to reach out to her and I wanted to stay far away. I settled for not moving at all.

"All it would have done is distract you. The best way to solve the problem was to get Mathilde and Dermot together. So, no, when I figured out that simple rescinding wouldn't work, I decided to say nothing."

I let out a low grumble and turned away from the window, running my hands through my hair and trying to figure out what exactly I should do next. I looked to Agravane, his expression still exhausted. I wanted to ask him for assistance, but I knew I shouldn't. This wasn't his battle. It was mine. I was his boss. And, he was already worn out. Ultimately, Agravane could tell me nothing more than I already knew. I had to do one dangerous thing to prevent another. If I didn't do this, then our whole reason for venturing to the mortal realm could be a risk. People could die. Agravane had left the order of silence to prevent such a thing. I didn't need to know his answer, because I already had it.

"Tell me this ritual. Tell me how to make a wish." I looked over my shoulder at Neja, her form eliminated in the lights from the city. She bowed her head.

"The ritual is not the hard part. The hard part is knowing the precise words with which to make the wish. But, I will start with the ritual. It requires fire, sand, and moonlight." Neja ran through the rest of the ritual, explaining the words in the payment that I must make. I had no idea what I could offer in exchange for a wish, but she said that she had a payment in mind it would work out just fine. But no one would get hurt. The hard part was finding sand and a place to set a fire.

In the end, the three of us went on a journey to the shores of the Great Lakes. At this time of night, or rather morning, there was no one else around except the few people patrolling the area to make sure that others didn't do something incredibly stupid. I think our task probably fell into that category.

"Don't you know anything about setting fire?" I snapped as Agravane broke our last match in half. He huffed and threw the pieces at me, sitting back on his heels.

"Setting fires wasn't really in the training manual. Just killing people. Besides, fire magic is one of the most simple things to do in Elsewhere." Agravane glared at me, but I didn't apologise. I needed to get this done right. Given that we were out in the open, the only thing that could crush me was a plane falling from the sky. With my luck, it would be a passenger jet. We needed to get this done now, and I didn't have time to coddle Agravane, to make sure that he was feeling pleased with his efforts, to train him.

I picked up the broken match pieces, striking the head against the box and getting sparks far too close to my fingers. The flame caught and before I could burn myself, I held it against the kindling of the tiny fire that I had built. A one month venture into the scouting as a boy had perhaps imparted something important. The fire took. I sit back on my own heels and grinned Agravane, who was, to my surprise, also grinning.

"You're not going to try and talk me out of this?" I asked, figuring I'd better ask just once. Agravane shook his head and shrugged, waving his hands so a warm breeze fed the fire. I supposed that having an air elemental hanging around was useful, not just for keeping me sane.

"Yolanda would have. She would be afraid that you would set about causing more problems than not. She would be equally afraid that someone would get hurt if you didn't do this. As far as I figure, you know what you're doing. They say that you don't know anything about Elsewhere, but I think you know more than you let on. You're not dumb." Agravane nodded firmly. Without another word, he rose to his feet and strode off a few paces so that he wouldn't get caught up in whatever residual magic I was summoning that evening.

"Thank you, I think?" I saw the flash of anger and smile in the dark, his eyes glowing almost like Neja's in the firelight. The breeze feeding the fire grew sharper, bringing with it some of the cold air off the lake.

I fished the flashlight out of my pocket, our impromptu substitute for moonlight. It was rather a cloudy night, though thankfully the rain had stopped and didn't make this any harder than it had to be. "You sure this is going to work?"

"It's the idea more than the fact that matters," Neja said, standing about twenty feet away she wouldn't interfere with the initial ritual. Apparently having a djinn show up to enact a ritual involving a djinn was like asking the chicken which came before the egg. Paradoxical and impossible. So she kept her distance. "Just sprinkle the sand and say the words while holding the flashlight."

I held up the flashlight and pointed it at the fire, its weak light doing not a whole lot. In my brain, I held an image of the moon, pretending that the light shining from my flashlight was in fact coming from the sky. In my other hand, I scooped up some sand and then sprinkled it into the fire, the flames crackling blue even as Agravane's breeze died away.

"From the sands of time in the shadows of lore, I call upon spirits of ash so that they might hear my call and heed my desires. A wish, a wish, a wish. For a price, a wish upon the moon that shines in the flames.

For as I seek to change that which is that which is not, so was the ash born of light and sand."

I repeated the words once more, then waited. To me, that didn't sound like much of a ritual, but then this was my first time performing true magic, and I would be the first to admit that I really had no idea what I was doing. Neja had promised me that this was but one of several different rituals of varying complications that would summon a djinn. The bargaining was apparently the really difficult part. This one some of that which is closest, disregarding the fact of whether it was benevolent or malignant or neutral. Since Neja was standing right there, there was nothing more but a flash of smoke, and then she was standing in the middle of the fire, the flames brushing against her skin and making the blue grey glow in the night.

Her hair was suddenly unbound, moving like the flames. Her eyes were brighter, glowing like a predator's in the dark. She held out a hand to me, flames dancing on the tips of her fingers. "You have summoned the spirits of ash, born of smoke and sand and moonlight. What price would you pay for a wish?"

This was the second part of the ritual, and she had told me what to say, though I didn't like it. To be fair, I had to admit that a lot of what had happened in the last twenty-four hours was really high on my didn't like scale. I wasn't really having a great time. So I said the words.

"For you, O great one, the price is yours to demand." Neja's eyes flared, some of the fire from her fingers leaping to the order and making her all the more terrifying. Her teeth had sharpened the points and I could swear that her hair was turning into smoke.

"You have honoured me, human. For that, my price shall be this. Upon three evenings following your returns Elsewhere, you shall have me over for dinner."

I coughed. "Seriously? That's your price? You want to go on a date? Well sheesh, I didn't need a wish ritual to ask you out."

Somewhere in the distance, I could have sworn I heard Agravane smothering a laugh. I promised myself that I would strangle him later, just as soon as he taught me how to fight. It was only fair after all. Neja, standing in the flames, rolled her eyes, the effect a little terrifying given that her eyes were now fully on fire.

"Do you accept the price or not, human?" She demanded, her voice taking on a double timbre.

"Well yeah. Absolutely." I was glad for the firelight, because I was fairly certain that I was turning bright red, and that was not a look that told of my intelligence or prowess. I wanted to look at least a little dignified since I was now contracted to take Neja out. I guess that saved me the bother of the awkward conversation at the end of all of this. I mean, technically, she had asked first.

Neja held out her hand, flames dancing from the fingertips, and I had to remind myself of the seriousness of the current situation. Date aside, the ritual was important. I had to take it seriously. So I held out my hand and clasped fingers with Neja, feeling my skin blistering and burning where the flames looked at them. When a drop my blood splattered onto the fire, the flames winked out, leaving Neja standing in their place as though they had never been.

"You have one wish, Cal."

She had explained to me that this was different than the whole three wish situation. That was usually reserved for beings trapped into servitude. Great sorcerers who had been turned into djinns by poor wishing. Demons, bound to an object for eternity. The alternative was for me to perform a good deed on behalf of a djinn, but that required some sort of animal and a few other things that we didn't really have. So I had summoned her. And paid a price.

The phrasing of the wish was one thing I had thought long and hard about. I knew precisely what to say and how to say it so that there would be no loopholes, no innocent bystanders getting hurt as I undid Matilda's wish. I opened my mouth to speak, and then something happened.

Much like the party, where Al had slipped in and taken control for that brief moment, catching me unawares and throwing the stuffed pepper at the Taxman, he stepped in and took control. Only this time, he pushed past my mental blocks and appeared from the shadows though he had always been there and I had just forgotten about him.

had forgotten. I had thought that I had locked him away in the recesses of my mind, that we had come to an understanding and that he was bound, but this was wrong. Al hadn't been bound at all. He had simply been waiting. And I provided him with the one opportunity to do exactly as he wished.

"I wish that the owner of the soul currently bound to Cal Thorpe's body to be regained of life and limb so that he might walk upon the earth and return to power in this time and this realm."

Neja's eyes widened. Agravane let out a curse and lunged towards me. It was too late.

The wish magic acted, and a flash of light, the incorporeal Al Capone that I had been seeing since I had taken possession of his soul, became corporeal. The emotions that had coursed through me, keeping me bound and saying in this reality, gave me functioning and normal instead of a hyperrational emotionless zombie, faded. I felt nothing but a mere interest in the situation, all shock and surprise, all fear and terror gone.

Agravane slammed into me, my head bouncing off some of the rocks on the beach, my skull fracturing and crushing beneath his attack. A moment later and my world went white, returning to dim early morning shadows a few moments later. By that time, Agravane was up and running after a form on the beach. Capone, I imagined. It appeared that the few moments it had taken Agravane to climb off of me and run after Capone had been enough for him to escape. Even an aurai trained in the art of balance between Life and Death, fighting and killing, could do nothing against the reinvigoration of the soul brought back to life.

Especially not the soul of Al Capone.

BACK TAXES OWED

"What was that?!" Neja demanded after we had all taken a moment to catch her breath. Al Capone was long gone, disappeared into the city. I lay back on the beach, looking up at the sky, wondering whether or not anyone would get mad at me for laying here all day.

Agravane was suddenly in my field of vision, and he reached down to pull me to my feet. I brushed myself off and then watched him curiously. Agravane sighed and ran a hand through his hair.

"That was...Al Capone. Cal had gained temporary possession of his soul due to the fact that he is currently without one, and it appears that Al Capone managed to gain control of Cal's body long enough to steal his wish." Agravane flashed an apologetic smile at Neja, who was standing on the beach with her fists clenched at her side, her eyes still flashing with fire.

She looked at me, raising her brows. "You don't

have a soul? How does a human lose possession of his soul?"

I blinked languidly, admiring the artistic symmetry of her jaw and wondering why it was that everyone seemed to be so upset. Logically, I knew the reason for it, but it did not seem to be cause for such rabid concern. I also knew that without a soul, my emotional response was greatly diminished, but I did not think it relevant to the situation at hand.

Once again, Agravane answered. "Death accidentally lost his soul when Cal was sent to the past by Time. The side effects get worse the longer he is without a soul. Right now, he's at the emotional capacity of your basic Vulcan. All logic, no emotion. In a day or so, even the logic will fail. You will have to order him to do simple things like grooming and eating. He will do them, without complaint, but he will not be able to do them on his own, of his own volition."

Neja took a step forward until she was standing just in front of me, looking up at me and narrowing her eyes. I blinked again, waiting for her to say or do something. She let out a huff and threw her hands in the air, turning and walking towards Agravane. "You know how dangerous soul binding is? If you don't have complete control over the binding, emotional or otherwise, then the borrowed soul can do...Well it can do exactly what just happened. Take control. How do we know he hasn't been possessed this whole time?"

"He hasn't been possessed because he's been acting like Cal, for the most part." Agravane walked over to me and put a hand on my shoulder, fixing me with an uncertain smile. Was I meant to respond? I did not see a need. The two of them seemed to be sorting out the situation optimally. "Trust me. It would take a lot stronger soul than Al Capone to gain complete control over Cal. He's stubborn."

Were they just going to continue discussing my current situation? It seemed to me that all the pertinent facts had been presented, and if my knowledge of the current situation was accurate, it seemed as though we should perhaps not let Al Capone wandered around. The ramifications on modern-day mortal realm society would be immense. I decided that it was time I spoke.

"As the situation appears, it would be prudent to recapture Al Capone and undo what has been done." Agravane frowned, and Neja winced. This was not the reaction I was expecting, given the fact that I had presented. Surely this was not news.

"He sounds terrible," Neja said. Ah. I understood.

"You are referring to the fact that I am not at present displaying any emotions common to the human existence. This is true. However, it is not currently relevant. If you would please focus your attention on the current problem, that would be beneficial." Agravane heaved a dramatic sigh and shook his head, wandering towards the edge of the beach where it bordered with concrete. Neja fixed me with a confused look, then waved a hand in front of my eyes, as if testing my vision.

"You're right. He's just like a Vulcan from Star Trek. Or a creepy psychopath. That's a really weird." She chuckled, though it appeared to me that the act of doing so did not alleviate any of her anxiety.

"This is not presenting any solutions to the problem of having Al Capone loose on the streets of Chicago. Do you not agree that this is problematic? Have I misunderstood the situation?" I waited for Neja to respond, hoping that she would provide useful insight into the situation rather than just pontificating on the fact that I was not as I had been. Instead, she sighed and threaded her arm through mine, leading me after Agravane and towards the parking lot.

"No, you have understood the situation correctly. The problem is that neither Agravane nor myself have any idea how to find Al Capone. Do you have any notion of how large Chicago is?" Neja's voice displayed a certain amount of emotional stress, and I gathered that the situation was suitably dire. I patted her hand, the action seeming to alleviate some of her stress.

"It appears to me that since Al Capone is only aware of the current situation within Chicago due to trailing along as my temporary soul, he is unlikely to deviate terribly from the path that we have followed and the people that we have met. As such, it seems most logical to assume that he is going to interact in some way with someone we have met. He is unlikely to speak with the American federal government, which limits our options to Mr. Green or the employees of Mr. Green. As Mr. Green is shortly to be giving up his profession in the world of organised crime to join the witness protection program, I would venture to say that Al Capone is most likely with his employees. Therefore, if we call Mr. Green, we should be able to locate him relatively quickly."

As soon as I had finished, Neja stopped walking, her jaw dropped open as she stared at me. Agravane stepped up next to her and patted her comfortingly on the shoulder, an act which seemed as though it should have drawn an emotional response from me, but which simply made me furrow brows and frown instead.

"Wow, that's..." Neja said. Agravane nodded, looking solemn.

"Yep. It turns out, that Cal is actually a whole lot smarter than we give him credit for. He just tends to overreact a bit and those smarts don't always show through unless he is without a soul. Don't worry, he'll be back to his normal self before too very long, providing that we can undo this whole mess with Capone." Agravane looked at me for a long moment, then shook his head, turning towards the parking lot. I followed, Neja trailing behind both of us. "I've got a ride on the way."

"Acceptable." I stood beside Agravane and waited patiently for the ride share to arrive. It was quite convenient when your assistant could anticipate your needs. I told him so. "It appears that I have done suitably well in training you."

Agravane snorted and shook his head. "Yeah, right. Because that's what happened."

While we waited for the car to arrive, Neja paced a bit, folding her arms and muttering to herself. After a few moments of this, she turned and walked towards us as though uncertain. Her shoulders were hunched and her eyes seemed larger than usual. Again, it occurred to me that this should evoke some sort of emotional response, possibly protectiveness or something along those lines, but I wasn't quite sure why or what the response should be. Eventually, she stepped between Agravane and myself, leaning towards Agravane and whispering to him, though the words carried far enough for me to hear. I wasn't sure why she was keen on me not hearing them, as I was not going to chastise her one way or another.

"The thing is, I'm not sure how to fix this. This is wish magic. It's the same situation we've been dealing with since Mathilde wanted to kill Cal by accident. The only way that it can be undone is with another wish, and at this point, I don't think that would be a good idea." Neja's eyes darted to me, perhaps gauging my facial expression for some form of response. I considered the problem, trying to come up with a solution.

"You have an accurate point. It seems unlikely that Al Capone would willingly rescind his soul, and I am unsure as to another solution that would achieve the same result. It occurs to me that perhaps the best option would be to capture Mr. Capone until such time as we can present him to Life and Death, who are more suited to sorting out such situations." I felt that my response was a good one, presented a valid solution to the problem. In return however, Neja and Agravane simply gaped at me and then turned back to one another to continue to whisper between them.

"That would be bad. Getting Life and Death involved is like bringing...It's like bringing a dragon to a discussion between rock trolls," Agravane said. I frowned, not understanding the metaphor, then nodded as a solution came to me. It would be, in colloquial terms, like bringing a gun to a knife fight. Or something along those lines, though the power of Life and Death seemed considerably stronger to me than the relative power of a gun over a knife.

"Well, I have no idea. This whole situation, this whole last couple of days, has been some of the strangest in my life." Neja gave another one of those chuckles that seemed as though its purpose was to reduce stress or anxiety as opposed to expressing amusement. Once again, the impulse struck me to reach out and pat her arm in some sort of comforting gesture. I gave into the impulse and received strange looks from both Neja and Agravane. Perhaps the impulse was a false one.

"Yeah, Agravane said, his chuckle seeming to actually express amusement as opposed to any other emotional relief, "things with Cal sure are strange. But they are never boring."

"Interesting. Are you suggesting that my presence enacts unusual circumstances that would ordinarily not happen otherwise?" I considered the implications, not quite sure what it meant. A car pulled up to the curb, the driver flushing the headlights at us. I followed Agravane as he walked towards the car.

"Yes, boss, that is exactly what I'm suggesting. Now get in the car and let's go find ourselves a mobster."

I decided that arguing would be nothing more than a waste of time and completely irrelevant. So I simply complied and got in the car, Neja and Agravane sliding in after me. Agravane gave the address to Mr. Green's apartment to the driver, and then we were off.

The car ride was spent in silence, each of us musing on our own thoughts, or perhaps deciding that it would be unfortunate should this perfectly normal mortal human male learn about our plans involving a fetch mobster and the reincarnated person of Al Capone. I wondered why it was that none of the humans seemed to comment on Neja's appearance. She never seemed to wear a guise, but the driver did not even look twice at her. I wondered if there was some sort of natural guard against humans for those denizens of Elsewhere who lived in the mortal realms more than they did Elsewhere. I was about to ask her about it when she put her hand over my mouth.

"Whatever it is, don't. I could feel you staring at me. Let's just get through our current crisis before we have to figure out a future one." Neja appeared exasperated with me and I was unsure as to the cause. I thought back over our interactions this morning and yesterday. Perhaps it was due to the fact that I had lost the temporary soul that was giving me human emotions and personality shortly after agreeing to go on a date with her as the price for the wish. I dismissed the thought a moment later, as it was completely irrational.

Some twenty minutes later, we arrived at the building of Dermot Green. We climbed out of the car, Agravane thanked the driver, then we walked up to the building, to be met by the doorman. It seems that this was the same doorman as yesterday morning, as he recognised us and sent us up to Dermot's apartment without a single word of protest. I followed Neja and Agravane up to Dermot's apartment and waited while Agravane pounded on the door.

"It seems to me that you are more likely to get a rapid response if you telephone rather than pound on the door," I said. Agravane paused in his knocking to stare at me. I nodded, asserting my sureness and my words. Agravane huffed and shook his head, then turned around and pounded harder on the door, the noise surely disturbing more than just Mr. Green. Luckily, before any of the neighbours could waken and ask us to explain our business, Dermot opened the door.

He was dishevelled, his hair sticking up at unusual angles and his attire simply a pair of boxer shorts. Behind him, a female figure waited, wrapped in a man's shirt with her mouth opened and poised to scream. As she was a banshee, this was a valid method of defence.

"Good morning Mr. Green," I said, stepping past him and into the apartment. Normally, rudeness was and not a logical act, but at this point it seemed more prudent than otherwise to explain the situation expediently. I ignored the wide-eyed stare that Mr. Green and his wife gave us as we walked inside. The door clicked behind us and we three went to the large table. I sat and folded my hands in front of me, waiting for the others to do the same. They did, not saying anything.

"It is useful that your wife is here, as it may be prudent to have more resources devoted to the current situation than otherwise. I assume that her presence indicates your relationship is on the mend," I said, nodding at Mathilde as she stared at me with open confusion.

"What is going on?" Dermot asked.

"We apologise for bothering you so early in the morning, but there has been an incident. Your wife," Agravane said, gesturing to Mathilde, who leaned back in her chair and folded her arms, "has unintentionally enacted a death wish against Cal. It was originally directed…at something else, but he got caught up in the crossfire."

Mathilde's face turned an intriguing shade of red. I was going to comment on it, but Neja slapped my hand as soon as my mouth opened. This seems to indicate that I should keep quiet, so I did.

"A death wish… What?" Dermot shook his head and looked at his wife. "Oh, you mean the one that was meant for me, don't you?"

She folded her arms tighter and looked pointedly away.

"This was before… Before you were back in my life, before things were going so well. I mean, of course I was glad that it hadn't actually worked, but was I to know that someone else would get caught up in it?" Mathilde sniffed and lifted her chin. Dermot blinked twice, then seemed to finally understand that having a death wish pointed your way was not, as it were, a compliment. He was not perhaps as unintelligent as I had originally thought. Then, I considered, he was technically still the boss of a criminal family and

Empire so it would be logical that he was not unintelligent.

"You put a death wish on me!" Dermot jabbed his finger into the table. "An actual death wish, not just some pseudo curse?!"

"Actually, no. Mathilde was imprecise in her wishing, and she simply pointed in your general direction before saying the words 'I wish him crushed dead'," Neja said. Her voice was flat, as though she disapproved of imprecision in wish making. Given that such imprecision was the cause of our current situation, I could imagine how carefully choosing one's words would be useful. "In actuality, she pointed at Cal. An accident, but problematic, especially since Cal cannot die."

"I can't believe this! You *actually* wanted me dead?!" Dermot stared in disbelief at his wife. She shrank into her chair.

"This was before. Before things got better, before you told me how you feel." Mathilde reached out to grab Dermot's hand, wincing as he pulled away. "You are being so distant, so mean, as if you wanted me to go far, far away. We've been arguing for six months, having to get lawyers involved in everything."

This time, I managed to provide the relevant facts on the situation before Neja could stop me. "In point of fact, Mr. Green was acting distant and pushing you away because he was working with the American federal government to go into the witness protection program, preparing to testify against his current colleagues and employees and therefore bring down his empire. As you were having difficulties, it seemed advisable not to inform you."

Everyone turned to stare at me, though I did not understand why. Neja hissed through her teeth and smacked my hand again, this time harder. I frowned.

"You were going to go into wit sec and leave me?!" Mathilde surged out of her chair, her voice reaching the particular scale of banshee ability that was likely to cause hearing damage with prolonged exposure.

Dermot cringed back into his chair, this time looking apologetic. "We were having problems. There was that guy that you are interested in and I was angry and..."

"It seems to me, Agravane said, sounding both calm and assured, "that both of you have made some rather profound mistakes in this relationship. However, things were going well this evening, so don't you forget that feeling. As it turns out, we are here for an entirely different reason. The wish magic that Mathilde sent against you, was redirected towards Cal. In attempting to undo that magic, we were forced to perform another wish. However, as Cal was using Al Capone's soul temporarily, he managed to gain control and is now corporeal and running around Chicago."

Once again, everyone was staring, though this time it Agravane. Neja and I said nothing, me because all the pertinent facts had been relayed, and Neja because, well, I do not precisely know, but I suspect it was also because all pertinent facts have been relayed. Dermot spluttered for a moment, coming to grips with the reality that we had just presented.

"Al Capone, the original mobster, is running around Chicago?" His voice changed pitch half an octave by the end of the question, a common indicator of distress.

I nodded reassuringly. "This is accurate. As it would be unwise to allow Al Capone free rein of the modern world, we must apprehend him. It is most likely, given the events of the past twenty-four hours, that he is in close proximity with the employees of your criminal enterprise. I would suggest that he is planning to take over your gang as you are going to leave it for the witness protection program. Therefore, I require information on where to find your people, as it is unlikely they are at the warehouse as we left there not some two hours before now."

Dermot put his head in his hands, staring at the table as if tracing the wood grain. "All of this is happening because it didn't pay my taxes."

I considered his statement, tilting my head as I processed the implications. "This is accurate. Perhaps we should see to recapturing Al Capone before we go about selling repayment of your back taxes. That is, I assume you and your wife are suitably interacting to convince a judge to release your funds? If so, this is good."

Dermot exchanged a strained glance with Mathilde, who looked, admittedly, a little green. Agravane rubbed his temple, muttering under his breath about difficult bosses. Neja snickered, fighting the expression in hand. I waited until Dermot pushed back from the table, wandering over to go grab his cell phone charging on the kitchen countertop.

"I'll call Ricky. The feds are going to be pissed, but I'll call him."

Mathilde also stood, pointing at Dermot. "After you do that, we need to have a discussion about your plans for the witness protection program."

TAX GUY

*D*ermot dialled the number on his phone and was just about to hit call when he turned to look at me. "You do realise that Agent Ferris is going to be beyond angry that I got in contact with Ricky again?"

"Considering that you are preventing a rival mobster—no need to mention that he happens to be from history—from taking over your enterprise, I would think that Ferris would forgive the lapse in the communication silence." I nodded my head at the phone, and Dermot looked down at the device, its glowing screen illuminating his features in the predawn light. He did not hit the call button.

"It's just that she was rather angry at me already this evening, for getting pulled in by Ricky. And that wasn't even my fault. She has questioned my dedication to our agreement, even threatened to put me into protective custody until everything went through. Given that we are in this situation because of my back taxes, I just want to be sure that you understand what is at stake." I believe that the tone and Dermot was using would be classified as menacing in a situation where I was able to feel fear. As I wasn't, and the extra deep growl at the back of his words did not particularly disturb me, I ignored it.

"I am perfectly aware of the circumstances. I am also perfectly aware that you are concerned about the fact that should things go wrong, you will be facing potential retribution by the Taxman. This is possible, but should things go well in dealing with your almost former lieutenant and Al Capone, then I do not foresee any potential issues in your tax situation." I nodded again at Dermot's phone, putting on a smile since I recalled from the time when I had emotions that people found them encouraging. Everyone winced.

Agravane leaned forward and shook his head, a grimace plane. "I wouldn't smile, Cal. You do well enough when you are in possession of the soul, but without…It's just creepy."

I reached up to touch my face, feeling the muscles that contracted when smiling. "Interesting. I would not have expected that phenomenon to occur. The muscle movements are the same."

Neja reached out and grabbed my hand, the act meant to convey something, though I wasn't sure what. "Worry less about the phenomenon of emotional effects on your muscles later. Right now, we have other matters to attend."

"This is correct," I admitted. I removed the smile from my features and waited once more for Dermot to hit the call button. The fetch studied me for a moment, then did as was requested of him and called his lieutenant.

Dermot held the phone up to his ear and paced in the small circle while he waited for Ricky to answer. "Ricky!" Dermot flinched back and held the phone away from his year, a significant amount of noise coming from the other end of the line. "No, no, it was nothing. The feds just thought they could intimidate me into making a mistake. No, they don't know anything...Oh really? And do you even know who this guy is? That's absurd. He'd have to be some serious powerful sort from Elsewhere to even consider such a thing. Does he even have magic? I don't care what he says he knows, he can't back up his claims, then...What, you don't trust me now? Because of one raid by the feds? We had loads of those in the past. You just don't like this one because I was busy trying to win Mathilde back. Yeah, well you know what's good for you, you'll wait to make a decision until you've heard from my side of the table. Oh, really? You're just gonna accept this guy at his word, believe such a ludicrous story without any proof. We've been working together for years Ricky and you just can't toss me aside like yesterday's trash because some gangster claims to be the reincarnation of Al Capone, who has just spent time wandering around trapped inside an employee of Death? I've heard saner things from the dragonwort dealers. Yeah, we do have past, and you seem to be forgetting that. Who has been there to bail you out of every situation? Who has helped you in all of your doings? Who gave you that loan for that bakery you wanted? Me, that's who. If you know what's good for you, you'll tell me where you are so that I can come meet you. Then we can talk things out. Okay, great. See ya in a couple hours."

Dermot pulled the phone away from his ear and ended the call. I looked expectantly at him, my own phone at the ready to take down the address. Dermot wrapped his hand around his own phone and said nothing for a moment. Then, he pointed at me, brows drawn.

"You're not going to do anything to Ricky for get involved in this, are you? He and I, we have had some good times together." Dermot took a threatening step towards me. Mathilde wrapped her arm around his and held him back, something in her own expression loosening Dermot's tension.

"My interest is not with Ricky, nor with the other members of your enterprise. I only seek to return Al Capone to his previous state of being. However, your question does not make logical sense. You were prepared to walk away from Ricky and all of your criminal activities simply because you wanted to be done with the life and were unwilling to deal with his questions and nagging on the situation, I believe was your description of matters. Given this, I am a little surprised at your apparent concern for him." Unlike the questions I had regarding facial muscles and emotional expression, I felt that this was a perfectly relevant question to ask. Apparently Agravane and Neja agreed with me, because they said nothing, both turning their heads to look at Dermot and wait for an answer.

Mathilde was the one who spoke. "You wanted to get out of the life?"

Dermot closed his eyes and sank down to the table. "I know full well that someone's status is determined by their power, by the influence they have, the people they control, the connections they make. But, for all the power that my work has given me, I am tired. There should be a point where I can retire to lounge on the beach and enjoy the success that my power has brought me without having to deal with the day-to-day business. The deal with the feds seemed like the most simple way to get that."

That, apparently, was not the answer that Mathilde wanted to hear. She fisted her hands on her hips, the shirt that she was wearing riding up to a level which I believe Agravane found uncomfortable. At least, he coughed pointedly and looked away. Neja simply smirked.

Mathilde leaned into the job that she directed at Dermot's chest. "If you're so keen on retiring, so keen on enjoying the few years that we have left, then why in the world were you in the life to begin with? Do you even care about the power? The responsibility? The respect? Why were you even doing this to begin with?"

Dermot did not even hesitate, he just reached out and grabbed Mathilde's hand, pulling her close despite the fact that she was rather angry and appeared to want to pace around the room. "I did it for you."

Mathilde blushed, turning a shade of red that was

actually quite impressive for someone who was not choking. She reached up and touched Dermot's cheek gently, then leaned forward and kissed him. It appeared to me that the two of them were going to increase their physical activity, and since we were rather in the middle of the situation, this did not appear to be the precise time for that. However, Neja was the one who coughed pointedly this time, causing Dermot and Mathilde to spring apart as though they were teenagers. Neja apparently found this amusing, because she snickered behind a hand.

"I appreciate that the two of you seem to be on increasingly better relational terms with one another," I started, "but I must impress upon you the urgency of the situation. The longer that Al Capone is allowed to wander around the mortal realms, the more dramatic his impact will be. And, as we are quickly approaching the early morning commute hours, I would suggest we get on the road before traffic increases."

Everyone was silent for a moment, once again staring in my direction. I was not entirely sure what it was that I had said to elicit such a reaction, but if it got the attention that was required, I would not complain.

"We'd better get his temporary soul back soon," Agravane said, his tone and expression displaying the typical markers of an explanation. "If we don't do so soon, he will start to focus on completely useless facts, and then he will do very little at all."

Dermot nodded, apparently reconciled to the fact that we were going to sort this out one way or another. He recited the address, which was to another property somewhere on the outskirts of the city. He said it was for a complex of apartment buildings that he owned, where he and his employees often stayed when they had to deal with some of the more's unsavoury aspects of the job. I rose as Agravane and Neja rose, following them to the street level where Dermot and Mathilde met us a few moments later, both fully dressed. Then, we had to deal with the problem of transportation. Mathilde assured us that she was not going to accompany us to the meeting, but would stay here and deal with the lawyers and the judge, waving a signed piece of paper in her hand as some sort of proof that Dermot agreed to everything. It took me a moment to see the relevance of her statement, but I then understood that she was referring to the situation with their finances being frozen, the entire reason for us being here to begin with.

It did not seem a terribly important thing, I will be honest. Then again, I wasn't entirely sure that taking down Ricky and Al Capone was any more important. However, I had set off on this path with the belief that it was important, so it seemed logical that it truly was. I would follow such instinct until such time as my faculties failed me and I required instructions on what to do and how to be. I knew that this would be problematic, that reacquiring a soul was one of my top priorities. But I could not bring myself to much care.

A few moments later, a taxi—a true taxi rather than a ride share—pulled up to the curb, the driver a young woman with the look of someone who had seen far too much in a short amount of time. Her eyes glinted with an extra colour, blue on violet. Given that the typical human genome did not display such colours, I gathered that she was another magical being. Agravane did not give me a chance to ask, nor to comment, he just opened the door and shoved me inside. Dermot sat up front and I thought sandwiched between Neja and Agravane, the taxi squealing away from the curb a few moments later.

"It smells of sage in here," I said. Neja took a deep breath through her nose and nodded. That was the only conversation that any of us had on the drive. It should maybe have struck me as significant, but did not. What did strike me as possibly significant was the way that Neja's hands clenched into fists on her knees, and grew tighter every few miles so we drove. By the time we reached the complex of buildings, she was looking drawn, her blue grey skin more grey than blue.

I turned away from studying her as soon as we stopped outside the complex. The buildings were tall and looked very much uniform, a set of blocks that had apartments with concrete balconies lining each floor. This was, I gathered, a typical source of low level housing that you would find in the city, well enough off as to provide a sense of security and safety, without having any of the extra frippery that places such as the hotel Agravane had booked for us contained. I tilted my head and wondered why it was that the image of the hotel stuck in my mind so strongly.

"Come along Cal, the party is this way." Agravane put his hands on my shoulders and steered me towards the central courtyard that stood between the three buildings. I walked dutifully, watching everything and noting such things as the small dogwood trees landed in the courtyard, the unevenness of the square cobbles, the fact that Ricky and Al Capone were standing right in the middle, bearing guns and other thugs with which to make themselves more impressive. Apparently, the earlier conversation that was had with Dermot did not preclude Ricky from seeming put out by whatever Al Capone had told him.

I imagine that whatever Al Capone had said, it was likely true. Al was a very capable liar, but he was not above using the truth when it suited him. I couldn't tell if I admired this or just found it interesting.

"Cal Thorpe," Al said, extending his arms in greeting. I remained where I was, unsure if I was meant to return the greeting or say something to the contrary. So I simply did nothing. Al blinked and lowered his arms, frowning. "Surely you can't be mad at me for this? After all, I only did what anyone would do. I got a second chance at life."

"I do not appear to be angry at you. Then, given that I am no longer in possession of the soul, I do not feel anything. However, I should inform you that Life is not always kind to those who would fight for her. She has a particular sense of fairness, and it does not often fall in the favour. of mortals." Having informed Al of the realities of Life, I felt that my duties had been discharged. Then, Agravane clapped me on the shoulder again and growled something low in my ear.

"Did you have a plan for undoing what he did?" Agravane glared at Al, who watched the aurai with mild interest. Ricky seemed far more interested in Dermot, but he did not interrupt the conversation that Al and I were having.

"Oh, yes. I am meant to undo his living. If you will grant me a few moments, I shall consider the matter." Agravane growled something else, though I did not hear what. He took a step back and left me to my thoughts. Meanwhile, Ricky took a hesitant step towards Dermot, his hand on the gun at his belt.

"Is what he says true, boss? Are you really gonna just give us up to the feds?" Ricky shifted his stance wider, more conducive to accurate shooting.

"No." Dermot straightened his shoulders, not looking intimidated by the presence of the gun. I wondered briefly if that was just posturing, but then I recalled Agravane asking me about a plan I went back to thinking. "After all we've been through, Ricky, you would believe that I would just give you up?"

"So why was the Fed lady nosing around earlier? Why did you go with her without a fight?" Ricky's voice trembled slightly.

"I went with her because you happened to have kidnapped me from the restaurant earlier. You can't do such things without consequences. You never could quite figure that out. Then, red caps are known for their love of blood, not their strategy. People notice if you kidnap someone, even if they are part of the same organisation. Or did you think that the manager wasn't going to call the cops?" Dermot curled his lip, straightening to his full height. A part of him seemed to shift, superimposing itself onto his skin, much like had occurred when I first met him. A death mask. The doppelgänger affect. As a fetch, this basically meant that Dermot thought someone was going to die.

I could not tell whether or not the image was of Ricky or of someone else. It did not particularly matter. I did not need Ricky to believe Dermot for this particular situation. All that had been required was for me to get in the same place as Al Capone. That had happened. And then I was supposed to do something...

"Cal," Agravane whispered, voice harsh. "We really need to do something now."

"What are you two whispering about?" Al narrowed his eyes. Ricky looked away from Dermot, instead focusing on Agravane and myself. He fingered his gun, then seems to think better of it.

"He says he's the tax guy. We got him in the warehouse. And then things fell, and he didn't...Dermot? Who is this guy? And tell the truth." Ricky's voice lost that tremulous quality. He seemed focused on me as a threat. And, more interestingly, he stepped between myself and Al Capone.

"Whatever you're going to do, do it quickly," Neja whispered, stepping closer to Agravane and myself. She looked even worse than before, her hands shaking slightly and a sheen of sweat on her for head, as if she were trying to control some part of her and doing poorly at it. I considered the implications and factored that into my calculations of the plan.

I had an idea.

I knew that the longer I waited, the less likely was going to be that I would actually execute that idea. I felt the lack of soul acutely, and knew, objectively, that my condition was deteriorating faster than it had before. I did not know if that was due to the fact that I was in the mortal realm, or that I was away from Death and Elsewhere and its magical properties, but it was happening faster. I did some short calculations and figured that I had perhaps two hours before I would become unwilling to do any action on my own. As it was, I felt apathy beginning to creep in and wondered once again why it was that I was bothering with this.

Then Ricky pulled his gun and pointed it at me, the tremor in his hand causing the weapon to waver between myself and Agravane, and I knew precisely why it was that I was doing this.

I stepped between Ricky and Agravane, moving closer to Al Capone.

"The way that I figure things, there are a couple of options for returning you to the state in which you previously were, that is, death. I could summon Death. I have done so before, and I am reasonably certain that he would heed my call as I do work for him. However, summoning Death would very likely also mean bringing Life into the situation, as you are currently a living being. This would start an argument between Life and Death, and I do not believe that we have suffi-cient time for such things. Besides which, such argu-ments can grow rather tedious for the mortals around them, as they more often than not end up disintegrated into several billion pieces. Naturally, as I cannot die, I would not be one to share that fate. It would be incon-venient, as I would have to find a new junior marketing agent and I have, I believe, grown accustomed to having Agravane present."

"Ah, thanks boss, you're my friend too." Agravane's voice held a note of sarcasm, which I ignored as it was not relevant to the situation.

I took another step closer to Ricky and Al, both of whom were watching me warily, but not retreating. I did not have a weapon and was therefore not particularly threatening. "The other potential solution to this situation would be that I simply kill you myself."

The weapons went up, pointing directly at me. Now, I was threatening. Interesting.

"However, I am not currently carrying a gun and I do not have a knife, either. I have never trained like Agravane, so I am unsure as to whether I would be successful in actually killing you with my bare hands before you managed to fight me off. After all, the only injuries from which I heal are the fatal ones, so I could very well be incapacitated before I achieved my goal, which would be inconvenient and annoying."

Al gave a nervous chuckle, only half of his mouth stretching in a smile. "So what are you going to do Cal? You don't seem inclined to let me run around. No matter that I got cheated out of my first chance at life. Arrested for tax evasion? Died in prison from syphilis? How is that fair?"

I shrugged. "My experience has been that Life is not fair at all. It does not mean that you should get a second chance. I believe the reason is that you were cast as the role of villain in history, and people are entitled to not experience that again."

Al pointed his gun directly at my head, though he was fully aware that I could not be killed. What a logical behaviour. I took another step forward. "So, what, you just gonna take me back to Elsewhere? Throw me back in that purgatory with Mata Hari and Genghis Khan?"

"No, as that would not solve the issue of me not having a soul. After all, there are still weeks left in our bargain. I am not to make another bargain until that time is up." By now, I was a mere few feet away from Ricky. He wisely jumped out of the way, cowering next to Dermot like the loyal lapdog that Dermot claimed he was. Apparently his doubts could not hold up to discussions of Life and Death. Then again, few people's doubts could.

Al took a step back, his features stretching in a grimace, making the scar across his cheek appear white. I believe he was expressing nervousness.

"Therefore, there is only one solution remaining to me. Neja's wish magic." I heard a sigh of relief behind me and imagine that Neja was doing her best to control the wish magic. That was the only reason I could think of for her being so strange in a situation which did not involve her except obliquely. At my words, she released some of her hold on it.

"Mathilde was pointing at you when she made the wish," Al said with a sneer, the gun once again pointed at my head.

I smiled, knowing that Agravane told me it was creepy, but sure that my muscle memory of such like-able smiles was perhaps strong enough to reassure Al.

Apparently, Agravane was right. Al looked even more alarmed and stepped back once again. I really should make a study of the impact of emotions upon the movement of facial muscles. It appears that moving the same muscles without the emotional intent was not effective.

I returned my focus to the matter at hand. "You forget, Al, that at the time I was in possession of your soul. As such, Mathilde was technically pointing at us both."

And then, Al blinked, and understood. He cursed, then fired the gun.

TAX RETURN ACCEPTED

Several decades being dead had not diminished Al Capone's ability with the gun. His shot rang true and hit me in the forehead, just a little to the left. My head snapped back and I experienced the familiar whiteness that came with one of my death experiences. When the world returned to me, I was on the ground staring up at the sky, my glasses a few feet away, the already cracked lens completely missing. Physically, I felt pain. But that was all I felt.

"Cal get up!" Agravane's voice echoed across the courtyard. I sighed and did as he said, thinking that perhaps it would be more worthwhile if I simply did nothing. But, I did have a task to fulfil. Being not dead would not push me back for long. I rose and grabbed my glasses from the ground, putting them on. As I did so, the world changed from an indistinct blur to a much clearer vision. What I saw was Al running away from me, moving towards one of the buildings.

I ran after him.

Before my encounter with Death that brought me into his employ, I was never a very good runner. My idea of exercise was more to do with brisk walks, the occasional yoga class, lifting some weights at home. After I had hired on with Death, I had learned the value of running and, being assured that my relative immortality meant that I would not experience the usual wear and tear that happened with running over time, I took up the sport. I was not particularly fast, nor was I particularly long-winded. But I was faster than Al.

I caught up with him about twenty feet from the entrance to one of the buildings. He turned over his shoulder to look at me and widened his eyes as I approached. Then, overestimating my ability and forgetting to calculate in the fact that I had previously been in a rather severe car accident trying to protect the FBI agent, I stumbled. Al gained three more feet. I stumbled again, my breath wheezing. But I managed to reach out and snag my arm on the back of Al's trousers. He stumbled, one foot catching on the uneven edge of a concrete block, then went down. I followed him.

Al was a much better fighter than he was a runner. He was scrappy, using his pugilist techniques and skills to deliver quick jabs to my nose and my glasses. My head snapped back, my glasses flying off my face once more. I decided that it was perhaps prudent that next time I got a pair of glasses to have them better fit to my face. The last two pairs had been loose and kept falling off. Perhaps it was a design flaw in glasses technology. I mean, surely there was a better alternative than wearing contacts, because sticking a finger in one's eye was distinctly annoying. But it seems that glasses were not designed for people who engaged in physical activity that—

Al hit me again, this time in the jaw, snapping my head to the right. I wrapped my own hands around his, pinning them to the ground. He got me in the back with a flailing knee. I moved one hand up to his throat, hoping to incapacitate him long enough for Neja's death magic to work. I certainly wouldn't be able to hold him long enough to actually kill him.

As I touched Al's skin, emotion rushed through me, pushing away the purely logical part of my brain that had taken over. It was almost as overwhelming as being hit several times in the jaw. And I felt furious.

This was a rage that burned through my veins, setting fire to my joints and making everything ache as I said about fixing the wrong that was done. I clenched my jaw, flashing my teeth like a predator, squeezing harder. Al spluttered beneath me, his free hand scratching at my face and neck. I snarled.

"Do you know what you have done?!" I demanded. Al shifted, loosening my grip on his neck. We scrabbled at each other for a moment until I managed to push my hand under his jaw, stretching his neck back.

"I did what anyone would have done under similar circumstances. I got a second chance. I don't care what you say about Life, there is no way I'm going to give it up." Al spoke through gritted teeth, my control of his jaw making it hard for his words to form. I wanted to slam his head into the concrete, wanted to see him dazed and suffering. I wanted to kill him with my bare hands.

The thought was shocking enough for me to pull back, releasing Al and ending our skin to skin contact. Immediately, the emotion vanished, leaving me back in the place of logic and fact.

His soul. I could still connect with his soul when we were touching our skin together. I simply needed to release him from his physical vessel to be able to regain control of his soul. Then, I could bind him more firmly to my will and this would all be over.

Al struggled beneath me, his weight shifting enough to push me off of him. I did not know enough about fighting to be able to keep my balance, just rolled onto the ground, scrambling to my feet as quickly as I could. Al had already started running towards the building again, the gun lying on the ground, forgotten. My previous injuries made it slow for me to move, slow to run after him.

But the brief contact with the soul had given me enough focus to know precisely why I was doing this instead of just letting him be. It wasn't because people didn't deserve a second chance at life. If anything, Life was fond of second, even third chances. It wasn't because he didn't deserve to try and right the wrongs. It was because I knew he wouldn't. Al didn't want to return to life to go about fixing the mistakes that he had made the first time. He only wanted to continue to gain power, to rule with an iron fist in the knowledge that he had gained after his death. He wanted what he had lost, and he was willing to step on whoever got in his way.

That was unacceptable.

I did not care that the reason I had come to Chicago was to deal with Dermot, a gangster who had likely done many of the same things that could be attributed to Al Capone. Illegal drugs, arms, prostitution, gambling. I had no doubt that Dermot was involved with all of it. I had come to collect Dermot's taxes, but I had a feeling that I had also been sent by both Death and the Taxman to right some wrongs. To alter the balance of the world so that Dermot's crimes might not cause so much damage. But the thing about Dermot that Al had not yet grasped, was that he did not care about the power, or the drugs, or the money. He had seen the effect that his life had on the people and he was willing to put it all away. Ostensibly because he wanted to retire, but also because he wanted to leave that particular life.

Al wanted to keep it.

Even without the emotion running through me that made me a distinct individual, that made me human, I knew that Al must be stopped.

So I ignored the pain. I ignored the fact that my ribs were killing me and that the bruises blooming on my back had flared to life after rolling on them during my scuffle with Al. I ignored the blood running down my face, the fact that I couldn't see particularly well. I ran after Al, I caught him, tackled him to the ground, and put my hand on his face.

The rage was still there, still pumping through my

blood. But I also felt fear. Terror of returning to waiting for the unknown. He had chosen to wait, rather than move on and see what was coming. He did not know what lay beyond, and he was afraid. The emotions were his, as well as mine.

"Why can't you just let me go? I can change." Al's eyes were pleading, his voice raspy. I shook my head.

"Maybe you can, maybe you can't. That's not the point Al. Capability isn't the point. It's whether you *will*. And you won't." I waited for Neja's death magic to hit us, hoping that it was not going to bring down a plane or injure innocent people in the process. Al started to tremble, his breath increasing until he was almost hyperventilating.

"I can't go back. I can just wait around never know. And I can't go on, either. This is my only option. Unless…What lies beyond?" Al's words became a whisper. I heard the cracking of something large, helped along by a warm summer breeze that's dirt up the air, the wind moving with just a hint of magic on it. Agravane.

I didn't look for whatever was coming to kill us. I just kept eye contact with Al. "I work for Death, not whatever lies beyond. Death is not God. Or a god. Or the devil. He is simply the release, the ferryman, the escape. From pain-and-suffering, love and sorrow. Death…You shouldn't fear it. I don't know what goes after. No matter how many times I die, I never get that far. But you shouldn't fear it."

Al gritted his teeth and shook his head. The breeze became a full windstorm, whipping the air around us and making the cracking sound louder. I continued to watch Al, keeping my attention on him. "You are a fool if you believe that," he said, shadows forming in his eyes. "Of all of the foolish things that you believe, like the goodness in people, the willingness for people to do as you ask, the willingness to do as they asked, to apologise for something that you *didn't even do*, this is the most foolish."

I sighed, the cracking growing ominously louder. The wind picked up so that my words could barely be heard, even by myself. "You allowed me to win the poker game because you wanted a chance to experience life. One more time. If you blame me for dooming you, then you should also blame yourself."

The only response I received in return was a snarl of disgust. Al turned away from me, the movement breaking our contact. For that brief moment when I still felt emotions, I was glad for the separation. Al's face twisted suddenly into a mask of fear, his brows drawn and raised together, his mouth dropping down in a circle of astonishment, a wail building in his throat. I was glad, for the brief moment of feeling that faded soon after, that I didn't have to feel Al when he died.

I twisted in the last moment, looking above me to see one of the concrete balconies of the apartment building break away from the wall, smaller stones dropping down around us, the larger pieces starting to crack. In a matter of heartbeats, the balcony fell down on both of us, crushing me and Al in a rush of physical agony.

The whiteness lasted longer this time, and I almost thought I could hear someone talking. Whispering my name.

A moment later and the world returned to me, dusty and dark with tracks of light shining through where the concrete had fallen. I coughed, dust flowing into my lungs. Above me, noises sifted through the rubble, people scrambling to pull it off of me. A couple of minutes later and I was free, being pulled from the wreckage by Agravane and Neja, their arms surprisingly gentle on my abraded skin. My earlier injuries, trebled by the balcony, had healed, the multiple fatal blows gone. All that was left was a few cuts on my skin and dust covering everything.

What remained of Al was considerably less pleasant.

"Is he…I mean…Do you have his soul again?" Neja asked.

I took a breath in through my nose, probing my thoughts and seeing if I felt anything. I didn't. There was no soul. Whatever Al had done had broken our bargain and left me bereft once again. It did not feel quite so urgent this time, perhaps some strange reprieve granted by the extra time I spend in the white. I turned to Neja, her eyes looking at me with some hopeful expression in the silver orbs. "No. I will require another solution."

Neja let out a wavering breath, then nodded. She slipped her arm through mine and helped me move away from the rubble while Agravane pulled out Al's broken body. We watched it for a moment, me trying desperately to see if I could feel some form of…something. Regret maybe? Relief perhaps? I wasn't entirely sure what I would feel in that moment even if I could feel. Instead, I just watched a few moments more, taking in the battered form of the tragic man. A few moments later and his body started to crumble away, disappearing into dust that flew off on the remnants of Agravane's air magic.

The three of us turned back to where Dermot and Ricky stood, having watched all of this with shock in their eyes. Ricky had somehow lost control of his gun, Dermot pointing it at his lieutenant instead. The red cap shook, his limbs looking as though they would barely help him to stay upright. Dermot, by comparison, was remarkably calm.

As we approached, Dermot looked at me for a few moments then nodded and turned to his lieutenant. "Ricky, I think it's time we moved on from the business. Both of us. Or do you honestly think that ending up like him will do you any good?"

Ricky trembled and swallowed nervously, looking over at his boss. He shook his head, saying nothing, mouth hanging open and slack-jawed horror.

Dermot lay a hand on Ricky's shoulder, lowering his head. "Go out there and do something productive with your life. I'm going to take Mathilde and we're going to retire to some tropical island somewhere. I think you should forget all about me, forget all about the life and the power that you wanted. There better ways to get it. Less…soul corrupting. Maybe paint your cap with the blood of criminals instead of the innocent?"

Ricky nodded dumbly, but I was not certain that any of Dermot's words were going to get through to the red cap. Generally speaking, emotionally traumatic incidents did not last in the mind very long. And the decisions made now, after witnessing such horrors, would be unlikely to have a lasting impact on Ricky's life unless he was truly intending to change. Witnessing such things did not always help someone grow for the better.

Or such was my experience.

Still, there was a slight chance that Ricky would take Dermot's words to heart. Of course, one could also consider the alternate interior motive that Dermot had in saying such things to Ricky, considering that he had already made a deal with the feds to disappear, having not hold his loyal employee of such. Convincing Ricky to leave the life, to not think about Dermot anymore would preclude such feelings of embarrassment or abandonment or betrayal.

Logically speaking, it was a very well played piece of manipulation. Unless it was sincere. I could not entirely tell.

Dermot turned to me, tucking the gun into the back of his waistband. We studied each other for a moment, and I wondered if I was meant to show some sort of emotion. After a few moments of debating whether or not I should attempt a smile again, Dermot shook his head. "It's been a very strange few days. Even before you arrived. Will things go back to normal after you leave?"

I considered, unsure if I had enough information to accurately answer the question. Thankfully, Agravane stepped in before I could explain the dilemma of answering the question to Dermot. The aurai slung his arm around my shoulder, earning a glare from Neja as she tightened her grip on me.

"That all depends on how you define normal," Agravane said. "Now, let's go get those funds sorted out so you can pay your taxes and we can be out of your hair."

Dermot nodded, fixed us with a wary smile, and we all walked to the edge of the curb to wait for a return trip to the city centre.

For a brief moment, even without my soul, I could've sworn that I felt...happy.

As if my soul were nearby.

TAX HOLIDAY

Come Saturday morning, Agravane, Neja and myself were standing on the curb outside of Dermot's apartment building, waving him farewell as he and Mathilde were ferried away by the US Marshals service. Agent Ferris stood near us, a cast on her left leg and an overall look of being rather tired.

She watched me as Dermot and Mathilde vanished into the interior of the US Marshal van. I have to say, I wasn't terribly sorry to see them go, especially not Mathilde, who had started complaining about what she could not bring on this rather permanent holiday. Even soulless as I was, I had found her annoying.

That was the other bizarre thing. Agravane and I had searched around the whole city of Chicago, spending most of Thursday and Friday searching for my soul. I would still get twinges of emotion every now and again—happiness, annoyance, pleasure, sadness—all very brief but very profound. And yet there was absolutely no sign of my soul, nor no indication that it had never been anywhere near Chicago and the mortal realm. Most of the time, I was acting purely logically, without emotion, based on the facts that I had at hand. I hadn't deteriorated into a useless zombie, nor had I reverted back to how it was when I first lost my soul: emotions wild and all over the place, some weaker than they should be, other stronger.

In short, I had absolutely no idea what was going on.

And I would have to wait until I could speak with Death before figuring it out. Of course, to do that, I had to deliver the check for a very large amount of money that was currently sitting in my pocket. We were meant to have given it to the axman the day before, but he had several meetings that were running late. Now, we stood on the curb with Agent Ferris, hoping that she left before the Taxman arrived.

"I did a background check on you, Cal Thorpe." Ferris's eyes narrowed, not making her any less distinguished. I waited. "According to all of my research, you are exactly who you say you are. Except for one thing. A Norwegian detective put in a report about a year ago about meeting a Cal Thorpe who claimed he worked for Interpol. There were some strange goings on in the report, and I could find out no more since the rest of it was classified beyond my clearance level. You wouldn't have anything to do with that, would you?"

"No," I said. The opposite was true. I had, in fact, been in Norway, chasing down leads on the murder of a jewel thief. Interpol had been my cover then, as tax auditor and the inspector was now. But I really didn't need Ferris asking any more questions. I didn't think she could handle what had actually transpired there.

Not yet, at least.

"Humph," she said. She turned back to watch as the Marshals made one last check on their vehicle, Mathilde's complaining voice sounding from inside. Idly, I wondered just how long their newfound bliss would last. My understanding was that this was not their first reconciliation. It was perhaps the most dramatic, but that could just be self-aggrandising on my part.

"Agent Ferris, may I make a suggestion," I said. She did not indicate the negative, but nor did she indicate the positive. I took her silence as permission to speak. "I imagine that an inquisitive nature serves you quite well in your chosen line of profession. However, might I suggest that in this instance you quell that instinct? It will not serve you any good to go asking questions when there are no answers. I am here as a representative of the Taxman, sent to retrieve the back taxes that Dermot Green owed. It is possible that I was also here in another capacity. But you will find no evidence as such, nor you will find anyone who knows anything. There are no answers. And, I acknowledge that it is very likely my saying such a thing will simply push you to seek out more answers, but I can assure you that I am telling the truth. You will find nothing, because there is nothing to be found."

Ferris bristled, and I imagine she would have stepped closer to him he had she not wearing a cast. As it was, she just clenched her fists at her side. "Are you threatening me?"

I tilted my head and blinked. "I do not know what I have said that would give you that impression."

She hesitated, then forcibly relaxed her muscles, keeping an eye on me as though she did not quite believe my words. I had not expected she would. Her behavioural patterns did not indicate that she was one who would easily back down. "You're different. There's something about you that...It's different."

She was, of course, referring to my lack of soul. The lack of emotion. Since I could not provide this to her as an answer, I simply inclined my head and walked away. When I looked back, Ferris was also walking in the opposite direction, moving towards the street so she could climb into the back of the waiting vehicle. The Marshal van had also pulled away, slipping into traffic as though it had never been there at all. I caught a glimpse of its bumper as it took a left turn and then it was gone, as if it had never been, and as if Dermot Green had never existed at all.

He had. And I would remember him, though perhaps not for the reason he would want.

The world shifted as I stood there beside Agravane and Neja, moving into the spectrum of black and grey, the colours leaching and the movement slowing as if the vibrancy in life that filled it was suddenly vanquished, or at least paused. I slipped my hand into my pockets.

"Hello Death," I said, voice perfectly flat, no twinge of emotion to acknowledge my boss's presence.

Agravane spun to face Death, standing directly behind him, a squeak escaping as he leapt back and lifted his hands in defence. His eyes were wide, terrified. A moment later and he relaxed, holding a hand to his chest and letting out a long breath. "Don't *do* that," Agravane said. "You scared me."

Death chuckled, the shadows wreathing around him seeming to echo the noise. "I do apologise, but your reactions are extraordinarily entertaining. Not even Yolanda makes that particular noise."

Agravane grumbled, but didn't say anything further. I stepped forward and put my hand on the small of Neja's back, moving her closer to Death.

"This is Neja. She is a djinn. Her death magic was enacted against me until such time as Al Capone died…again."

Death nodded his head in greeting to Neja, but he did not say anything.

I frowned, breathing in through my nose and letting out a slow breath. "There is really no good way to explain the events of the last few days simply. I suggest that if you wish for a full explanation that we sit down over a cup of coffee. I like coffee. I really like coffee."

Emotion surged in me at the mention of coffee, desire making my mouth water. A moment later and it was gone. Death sighed and shook his head. He reached into his jacket pocket and handed me a small parcel. I opened it and found a new pair of glasses, stylish and precisely fitted. I replaced the broken and smashed ones on my face with the new pair, nodding and affirmative when they matched my normal prescription.

They even fit better.

"I am aware of the events of the last few days. I was informed of such by the Taxman once he discovered that Al Capone was sharing your soul. He has been wary of Al Capone for many decades. That is one soul that sought too much, even after death." He pressed a hand to his chest, inclining his head. "Things did not go as I had anticipated. Al Capone retained far too much control, influencing through his emotions. It would seem that a borrowed soul is not your best option."

"I have been feeling emotions since Al Capone... died again. Is my soul nearby?" I straightened, some sort of excitement slithering up my spine. I was unsure if it had to do with Neja stepping closer to me, still eyeing Death warily, or if it was to do with the thought of being reunited with my soul. The emotion was gone too soon for me to understand.

"I do not believe so. If it were, I would've been able to locate it. I believe you are experiencing something similar to what happens when people lose a limb. They experience sensations, as if the limb were still there. I believe this is what you are experiencing. It is not a true soul, nor are the effects permanent. But they will prevent you from deteriorating further, at least until some other solution can be sought." Death watched me for a moment, then slid his eyes to Agravane and to Neja. A moment later in his gaze was back on me, those empty holes where his eyes were seeming to grow wider, showing a void that should not have existed.

"I have…Phantom soul syndrome?" I frowned.

"How long will it take to find his soul?" Neja asked, a slight waver in her voice. Death smiled at her, the sight making her stiffen and tighten her grip on my hand.

"There is no need to be afraid of me, djinn. You are a creature borne of smoke and ash and desire, as permanent as you are ephemeral. In terms of Elsewhere lingo, you are immortal. My effects on you are limited." Death held out a hand and some of his shadows moved from it to dance around Neja. A moment later and they returned to Death, Neja none the worse for wear. She did not seem reassured.

"That's not what I—"

"Nor do I disapprove your interest in Cal, though I cannot help but wonder if you are sincere in your motivations. A being like you is drawn to adventure, to excitement. In this time in this place, Cal provided both. He will not always do so. Do you wish to stake a formal claim, or are you simply going to play with him until you grow weary?" Death's voice took on a biting edge, one that I would have called protective had I been sure of the emotion there. It could have just as easily been curiosity.

However, the words had some effect on Neja. This time when she stiffened, she released my hand and took a step back, her eyes flitting between me and Death. A few seconds later and her expression shifted into that familiar smirk that she had worn so often when we first met. She shrugged, jutting a hip out and folding her arms. "They say no one escapes Death, but they do not say that you are perceptive."

"Many try very hard not to describe me at all," Death replied evenly.

Neja made a noise in the back of her throat then shook her head. She looked at me. "You still owe me dinner. Three days after you return to Elsewhere, I'll be there. After that, Cal, I wouldn't expect much."

Before I could say anything, even to ask what she was talking about, or her motivations, or anything, she spun on her heel and disappeared in a cloud of blue grey smoke. A few seconds later and even the cloud was gone.

"I apologise for that," Death said. "Djinns are more dangerous than you can imagine. One must be very clear about their motivations before engaging with them in any sort of manner. She could be quite sincere in her attachment. Or she could have some ulterior motive. Do you understand?"

I shook my head, the slightest touch of sadness whispering in my ear. But the streets of Chicago were quiet, no sign of Neja. "I don't. And I doubt I ever will...I have the check for Mr. Green's back taxes. The Taxman was meant to collect yesterday, but he had to delay due to some meetings."

Death held that his hand and I gave him the check, the paper feeling flimsy after all we had gone through to get it. "I shall see that he gets it. And Cal? I believe it's time for you to go home. I have to discuss a holiday with you."

A moment later and Death, too, was gone, though the world of Chicago remained firmly in the greys, the people in the cars were slowing down even more and fading into the background. The transition back to Elsewhere. I looked at Agravane as the last of the mortal world fell away and he shrugged.

"Maybe you'll get that holiday you've been wanting," he said. I doubted it. I had been wanting a holiday for rather a long time and it never seemed to happen. Still, it would be pleasant to sit in the countryside and have a nice cup of tea, doing very little for a couple of days. And yet the emotion that flitted through me as I thought about the possibility of a holiday, holiday, was not hope, but dread.

I wondered what that was about.

END, Book III

ACKNOWLEDGMENTS

I am always grateful for everyone who has helped make this journey happen. It is impossible for me to do this alone, and I want to thank everyone.

Firstly, I should like to thank my Grandad, Jim, who provided much of the inspiration for the premise of this book. I'm sorry you'll never be able to read this; you will be missed.

Next, I should like to thank my dad, who took my general thoughts about Death and The Taxman, and helped push that into the absurdity that it became. There's nothing quite like snarking about taxes to improve a novel.

Many thanks also to Fay Lane, who does the covers for these books. They are always stunning.

And perhaps most importantly, thank you to my readers for being there through all the weirdness that these books present. I appreciate your weirdness, because it matches my own.

ABOUT THE AUTHOR

E.G. Stone is an independent author who has been writing, creating and causing vast amounts of trouble since the age of six. Since then, E.G. has improved rather a lot in both the trouble-causing and writing and now spends her time writing fantasy and science fiction. When not writing, she is off musing about the workings of languages, both real and created, or drawing and sewing. E.G. reads voraciously, perhaps to the point of slight-insanity. Weird, nerdy, perhaps a little crazy, she is having a grand old time writing, reading, reviewing, interviewing, and, naturally, continuing her endeavours in causing trouble.